Bateman was a journalist in Northern Ireland before becoming a full-time writer. His first novel, *Divorcing Jack*, won the Betty Trask Prize, and all his novels have been critically acclaimed. He wrote the screenplays for the feature films *Divorcing Jack* and *Wild About Harry* and the popular BBC TV series *Murphy's Law* starring James Nesbitt. Bateman lives in Ireland with his family.

Praise for Bateman's novels:

'The funniest crime series around'   *Daily Telegraph*

'As sharp as a pint of snakebite'   *The Sunday Times*

'Sometimes brutal, often blackly humorous and always terrific'
Observer

'A delightfully subversive take on crime fiction done with love and affection. Read it and weep tears of laughter'
Sunday Express

'An extraordinary mix of plots and characters begging to be described as colourful, zany, absurd and surreal'   *The Times*

'A joy from start to finish . . . witty, fast-paced and throbbing with menace'   *Time Out*

'Twisty plots, outrageous deeds and outlandish characters, driven by a fantastic energy, imagination and sense of fun'
Irish Independent

'Bateman has barged fearlessly into the previously unsuspected middle ground b_____ ___ _____ Winson and Irvine Welsh and claimed i_____   *GQ*

'Extremel_____   *Loaded*

D0306560

By Bateman

Belfast Confidential
Cycle of Violence
Empire State
Maid of the Mist
Wild About Harry
Mohammed Maguire
Chapter and Verse
I Predict a Riot
Orpheus Rising

Mystery Man novels
Mystery Man
The Day of the Jack Russell
Dr. Yes
The Prisoner of Brenda

Martin Murphy novels
Murphy's Law
Murphy's Revenge

Dan Starkey novels
Divorcing Jack
Of Wee Sweetie Mice and Men
Turbulent Priests
Shooting Sean
The Horse with My Name
Driving Big Davie

For children
Reservoir Pups
Bring Me the Head of Oliver Plunkett
Titanic 2020: Cannibal City
The Seagulls Have Landed

MOHAMMED MAGUIRE

BATEMAN

headline

Copyright © 2001 Colin Bateman

The right of Colin Bateman to be identified as the Author of
the Work has been asserted by him in accordance with the
Copyright, Designs and Patents Act 1988.

First published in Great Britain in 2001 by
HarperCollins*Publishers*

First published in this paperback edition in 2013 by
HEADLINE PUBLISHING GROUP

1

Cataloguing in Publication Data is available from the British Library

ISBN 978 1 4722 0135 5

Typeset in Meridien by Palimpsest Book Production Limited,
Falkirk, Stirlingshire

Printed and bound in Great Britain by
CPI Group (UK) Ltd, Croydon CR0 4YY

Headline's policy is to use papers that are natural, renewable and
recyclable products and made from wood grown in sustainable forests.
The logging and manufacturing processes are expected to conform
to the environmental regulations of the country of origin.

HEADLINE PUBLISHING GROUP
An Hachette UK Company
338 Euston Road
London NW1 3BH

www.headline.co.uk
www.hachette.co.uk

For Andrea and Matthew

Prologue

Not for the first time that morning there was a child crying in Santa's grotto.

Santa, with his expansive girth and expansive mouth, and his chins covering a wide expanse of his expansive chest, snarled helplessly at her as she hurtled away across the cracked linoleum, screaming for Mummy. Then an elf whispered in his ear, 'There's something up, I can feel it in my water.'

'Yo friggin' ho,' Santa growled.

And there was. Upstairs, Mr Clarke sat with a bottle of whiskey, the receiver sitting off the hook on the desk before him, staring out of the window. He was on his fourth glass, four in fifteen minutes. Anyone's head would be spinning with this news, with the enormity of it. It was Christmas Eve.

He had been fingering the microphone for several minutes. *Christmas Eve!* He could see his staff on the monitors, diligently working, or at least diligently standing in the absence of a rush of customers, their green and red elf outfits suitably festive and suitably cheap. Mr Clarke's ability to cut corners was legendary, and even if he did have to replace the crêpe paper outfits at regular intervals it was still less expensive than investing in proper uniforms. Even when they did inevitably fall to pieces he was able to plaster the arms and legs all over the shop and cut back on needlessly expensive tinsel.

But was he congratulated? Was he hell.

The decision to close J.M. Huff and Sons, Belfast's leading toy store, on Christmas Eve was taken lightly. Or at least it seemed that way. Some nameless accountant in some nameless city across the Irish Sea had calculated that Christmas rush or no – and in fact it was no – the shops that formed part of the group that formed part of the chain that formed part of the multinational retail conglomerate had to close, and had to close *now*. On Christmas Eve. That, or the receivers would be brought in and they would lose everything.

Shut those tills.

Sack those staff.

Yes, we know it's Christmas. Just do your job. Not that you have one.

Mr Clarke switched on the microphone. 'Ladies and gentlemen,' he began, then coughed. Tears welled up in his eyes. Christmas Eve.

On the ground floor Mo was approaching one of the tills. An elf was behind it, filing her nails. Hardly anyone else was in the store, and the shelves were full. Two security guards stood chatting and smoking in the doorway. Mo carried a huge bear. Huge and £48.99. It was for Tar. For Christmas.

He put the bear on the counter and offered the

elf the money. She took a moment to finish off a nail, then smiled impatiently and put out her hand.

'Do you want it wrapped?' she felt obliged to say as she started to count.

Mo shook his head.

And then the PA crackled again and a moist, strained voice said, 'I regret to announce that due to difficult, nay impossible, trading circumstances, headquarters has ordered that this store be closed forthwith to prevent further losses.'

The elf looked at the ceiling. The security guards flicked ash on the floor and shrugged.

'All tills should be locked immediately.' Mr Clarke gripped the microphone a little harder. 'Customers, if there are any, would you kindly leave the store, and many thanks for your support over the years.' He cleared his throat. 'There will be a staff meeting . . .' his voice finally cracked, '. . . sometime.'

The elf pulled off her hat and rammed the cash drawer closed. She reached the money back to Mo. 'I'm sorry, sir,' she said, 'this position is now closed.'

'I've given you the money.'

'And I'm giving it to you back. Forty-eight ninety-nine.'

'I don't want it back. I want the bear. Ring it in. It won't make any difference to you.'

'I'm sorry, sir, I'm only following orders.'

'That's what they said at Auschwitz.'

She put her hand on the bear and began to pull it towards her. Mo retained his grip. 'It's Christmas, for Christ's sake,' he said.

'And Merry Christmas,' she said, 'but the bear stays.' She gave it a tug.

Mo tugged back. 'Don't be ridiculous.'

'I'm not the ridiculous one.' She gave it a good one, nearly got it, but Mo hung on and pulled even harder back and the bear came free in his hands.

'Sir!'

'It's *my* bear. Now are you gonna take my friggin' money?'

'No, sir.'

'Right.' He swiped the money off the counter and put it back in the pocket of his donkey jacket.

'Right,' he said again. He turned away from the counter, bear in hand. Two hands, in fact, it was a bloody big bear.

The security men were looking at him. One was grinding his cigarette into the ground, and the other wore white socks. Mo looked back at the elf. Her eyes narrowed, daring him.

He gave a little shrug and started to run.

'Security!' the elf shouted, and the chase was on.

Through the ground floor. Through Barbie and Barney and Rugrats and Bananas in Pyjamas and Noddy and Oakie Doke and then up the stairs to Star Wars and Star Trek and Jurassic Park and Toy Story, the security guards on his heels, Mo throwing everything back at them as he passed: footballs and rag dolls and life-sized cardboard cutouts of the Spice Girls. But they battled on; they hadn't had this much excitement in years, it didn't matter to them that they were no longer being paid for it.

Second floor and the administration offices. Mo ran on.

No Christmas up here. Dull blue walls, chipped and graffitied, closed doors, empty rooms. The security guards smashed through the swing doors behind him. Dead end. Him and the bear. He rattled the first door – locked. The second and third. They were nearly on him; he heaved his shoulder against a fourth and it gave way.

He was in a boardroom. A big table, a dozen chairs, a film of dust. He was on the far side of it, windows behind him looking over the city, the guards on the other side, puffing, holding out placatory hands, palms upward. 'Just put down the bear!'

Mo and the bear. The security guards, nicotine fingers, breathing hard. Mo stepped back. He reached up, his hand feeling blindly for and then grasping the window handle while he watched for any sudden moves. He pulled the handle. It opened, a draught of cold crisp air. He pulled himself up onto the window sill. The security guards, ashen-faced now, began to move round the table towards him. Mo and the bear stepped out onto the ledge.

He looked down.

It was a long way down.

The security guard, at the window now, said pretty much the same. 'Sir, please, it's a long way down!'

Mo took a deep breath, nodded and began to shuffle along the ledge.

A shadow passed behind Mr Clarke, but he did not notice. He had finished one bottle and was contemplating another. Then the door to his office shot open and there were two drop-jawed security men looking at him, and for a moment he feared that they'd been sent to remove him and his belongings, but then he saw they were not looking at him but beyond him and he swivelled in his chair and saw Mo, or Mo's back, or Mo's back and a bear, or Mo's back and a bear's back, moving past his window.

He was up out of his seat in a flash. He was the manager. The manager still. The manager still and pissed. The security guards were at the window already, but he pulled them back. 'Let me,' he said, 'let me.'

They stepped back. Nobody had said anything about window ledges when they were hired, so they were quite relieved.

Mr Clarke leant out of the window. The cool air hit him and he suddenly felt quite dizzy. He shook his head, which didn't help. He gave it several moments to clear, then bent out to look at Mo and his bear. Or Mo and *his* bear.

Mo, shivering already, back to wall, was staring at the ground.

'What the hell do you think you're playing at?' Mr Clarke said.

Startled, Mo nearly slipped. He turned his head. His eyes were wide and panicked. Mr Clarke's were small and bloodshot.

'What's it look like, you stupid bastard?' Mo shot. 'I just wanted to buy the friggin' bear – it's Christmas!'

'I know it's Christmas, but there's no need for this . . .'

'That's easy for you to say! My life's falling apart! And I can't even buy a friggin' bear without someone trying to arrest me!'

'You're not happy! *I'm* not happy! I've to sack forty-eight of my staff this afternoon, and it's Christmas for them too!'

Mo slumped back against the wall. There were tears in his eyes. Mr Clarke tried to hold back the tears as well.

Mo looked at the ground, way below. At the innocent shoppers and the fairy lights adorning the shop windows opposite. 'What's the point in it all?' he said weakly.

Mr Clarke climbed out onto the ledge.

'Keep back!' Mo yelled. 'Keep back! I'll jump! I swear to God I'll jump.'

'So jump. I'll follow you down. I've had enough of all this.'

Mo looked incredulously at Mr Clarke, then shuffled a bit further along to make room for him.

Down below the fire brigade arrived. Shoppers stopped to gawk. A child pulled her mother's arm and said, 'Look, Mum, jumpers!'

A newly unemployed elf turned to another and pointed to the top floor. 'Look – Mr Clarke!'

The other nodded sagely. 'He won't be handling the redundancy counselling then.'

On the ledge, Mr Clarke said, 'Is it just about the bear?'

'Don't try to analyse me!'

'I'm not! I'm not! I don't care! I'm only being polite.'

'We're about to kill ourselves, and you're being polite!'

Mr Clarke shook his head wearily. 'Death is no excuse for bad manners.'

They both looked at the growing audience below. The fire brigade was busy inflating something.

'We gotta keep moving,' Mo said, and they edged round the side of the building.

For the moment they were alone. Mo sighed. 'No,' he said, 'it's not just about the bear. It's . . .' He shook his head. 'You wouldn't understand.'

In Mr Clarke's office – his *former* office – the security guards had been joined by several uniformed police officers and some elves up to gloat. None of them knew quite what to do. They turned at the sound of heavy footsteps in the corridor, hoping it might be someone with the solution, but it was Santa.

Santa, in his cheap, ill-fitting uniform, with off-white cotton-wool beard hanging loose and red DM boots, snarled, 'Let me through, I'm a jolly mythical figure,' and they parted wordlessly before him. Santa popped his head out of the window, nodded at Mr Clarke and Mo as they reappeared around the corner, then climbed out onto the ledge. 'Do ye mind if I join ye?' he rasped.

'Don't try to talk me down!' Mo bellowed.

'Ach, jump for all I care, I'll see you down there.' Santa pressed his head back against the wall and closed his eyes.

'Oh God, Santa, you as well?' said Mr Clarke.

Santa took a deep breath and opened his eyes. They were red and raging. 'I'm sick to death of perpetuating a capitalist ploy to wrest every last penny from the hard-working proletariat,' he said.

'At least they have jobs,' Mr Clarke observed.

'How can you be Santa Claus if you're a friggin' communist?' Mo asked.

Santa fixed him with his stare. 'You have to become Santa before you can destroy him.'

And then he lost his footing and slipped down and was about to go over with screams already coming up from below when Mr Clarke just managed to grab him and hold him while Mo reached over and helped yank him back up by his baggy red shoulders.

There was a wave of *oooooh*s from below as Santa regained his feet, but there were no thanks. 'You should have let me go,' Santa growled.

He had a point. They were all up there for a reason. They looked at each other, and nodded.

'We should all go together,' said Mo.

They looked at each other again, nodded. 'United we fall, divided we stand,' said Santa.

Mo took a deep breath. 'Okay. Let's do it now. Let's go. Jump, and our problems are over. On the count of three.'

'One,' said Santa.

'Two,' said Mo.

'Wait!' said Mr Clarke.

They were at the *very* edge, bending over into the Christmas breeze. 'What!' said Mo.

'Why three?' said Mr Clarke. His teeth were chattering. 'Why not seven or ten or eleven?'

'It doesn't friggin' matter! Now c'mon! This isn't easy, y'know!'

'I know!'

'Now . . . one!'

'Two!' said Santa.

'Wait!' yelled Mr Clarke. *'Wait!'*

'What the frig is it now?' Santa demanded.

Breathing hard, Mr Clarke said, 'We can't just go one-two-three jump. We're going to look like hotheads.'

'And waiting for seven will make us look cool and calm and collected?' Mo jabbed a finger at the ground. 'Let's go!'

But now Santa was holding back. 'Wait . . . wait a moment. He has a point. You don't want people to say, Oi, did you hear three guys went mad and threw themselves off a tall building today. You want them to say, Hey, those three guys, they made a statement!'

'Yes!' said Mr Clarke. 'A statement!'

'Then they went mad and threw themselves off a tall building!' Mo couldn't believe it. He put his hands to his head, shook it, peered out between his fingers at the swelling crowd below, sighed deeply, then leant back against the wall. 'Okay. *Okay*. Have it your way. How long represents a statement?'

Mr Clarke looked at Santa, who looked back. Mr Clarke looked at the ground and the inflatable mattress and the elves who'd worked for him just a short while before, then at Mo's tear-stained face and sallow complexion and hollowed eyes, then Santa in his crap uniform. 'About half an hour?'

1

Libya, 1979

She ran, screaming, slowing with every stride as her feet sank further into the sand. He was gaining on her.

She began to zigzag, but it was too late; he was too fast. The pad of his feet on the North African desert was barely audible, and all the more intimidating for it.

He dived. His outstretched fingers just caught her heel as he hit the ground and she tumbled.

She was well trained; she went head over heels once and was back on her feet and running, barely losing a stride. From behind she heard him laugh. Within seconds he had closed the gap on her again.

She knew it was hopeless. Better to stand her ground now than exhaust her reserves running for it. She zigged once more, then stopped abruptly, turning on her heel, surprising him. As he clattered into her she fell back, expertly grabbing his uniform at the shoulders and kicking him up and over. He landed with a dull thud in the sand, the wind knocked from him. She dived for him, but he rolled sideways and she tasted sand in her mouth as she landed. Then he pounced.

He pushed her head back into the sand. As she tried to raise herself he pulled her feet from under her, slamming her flat. With one hand firmly clamped to her neck, he began to pull at her khaki trousers. She shifted left, then right, but she couldn't budge him. He got her trousers as far as her ankles but they became entangled in the tops of her black army boots. He pulled at each leg in turn, grunting in frustration as they refused to yield. Then he grabbed both trouser legs at once and yanked with all his strength, but still they stuck on the boots. Frustrated, he pounded his fist into the sand and let out a low animal howl.

Suddenly he released his hand from her neck and sat back.

Octavia Maguire giggled.

'Please,' he said, 'this joke, getting beyond.'

She giggled some more, then turned herself onto her back. She sat up and, squinting in the sun, smiled at him. 'It's not that difficult,' she said between heavy breaths, then reached forward. Using her thumb and forefinger she clasped one end of her left bootlace and pulled it delicately, as another woman might remove a silk glove at a society ball. The knot unfurled perfectly and she was able to kick the boot up into the air and catch it. She repeated the manoeuvre with the other boot; when she kicked it this time he reached up and caught it, sniffed it, then threw it contemptuously behind him.

'Now,' Octavia said, 'off with the trousers.'

At last he smiled. He pulled them off with one hand. Then he reached for her knickers.

An hour later they walked home hand in hand. Half a mile from the camp one of the guards rose up out of the sand, but when he recognised them he waved them on. Then as they came over the brow of the hill they stopped for a moment to observe their summer home.

Spread out beneath them were fifteen huts. They were basic in the extreme: a mix of scavenged wood, corrugated iron and Libyan army canvas. Octavia checked her watch. Although it was now moving into the pleasant cool of early evening there were only two or three figures to be seen about the camp.

'We'd better hurry,' she said.

Mohammed Salameh nodded then let go of her hand. Although they were recognised as partners, they kept even the most innocent of intimacies for the privacy of their romps in the surrounding desert, or for those few nights when the camp was sufficiently empty for them to sleep undisturbed in one of the huts.

As they jogged together into the central quadrangle one of the guards on the surrounding hills blew a whistle; they increased their speed then parted wordlessly as they approached their respective enclosures. As soon as they entered the doors were closed quickly behind them. Now they would spend thirty minutes in the dark while the CIA photo-reconnaissance satellite passed overhead. Then they would return to business.

There were nearly a hundred international terrorists present at that time, in that camp, some vastly experienced in their abstract theatre of war, others ambitious fledglings wanting to fly or at least to be trained in preventing others from doing so. They came from the Palestine Liberation Army and the Hizbollah in Lebanon; there were Kashmiri and Punjabi separatists, and members of the German Red Army Faction and the Red Brigade in Italy. And of course the Provisional IRA, for whom Octavia would shortly qualify for her fifteen-year membership badge. Octavia, born on the Falls Road in Republican West Belfast, had joined the IRA straight from school and had been attending Colonel Qaddafi's summer camps for over ten years. On her first year, a fledgling then herself, she had met and fallen in love with one of her instructors, Mohammed Salameh, now a leading figure in Sheikh Abdel Rahman's militant Egyptian fundamentalist group, Al-Gamaat Al-Islamia. Their affair had continued annually ever since, nearly twelve years now.

In the gloom of the hut Octavia did not realise for a few moments that *he* was not there. The five Irish lads she had brought with her this time were on the floor playing Monopoly. They had, of course, adapted the game to their own circumstances, re-evaluating the houses and hotels in terms of the economic loss the British economy would suffer if they were bombed. Chance cards now referred to the likelihood of apprehension by Scotland Yard. Terrifyingly few went straight to jail.

'Where's . . .?' she began, but her words suddenly trailed away as they all looked to the door. Outside: the dull thump of an explosion. Distant, but . . .

And closer.

The Monopoly board hit the floor and thousands in worthless cash floated briefly as the boys grabbed their weapons.

'Easy!' Octavia yelled. 'Easy!'

But they had their fledgling adrenaline and the door was open and they came spilling out into the quad before they were half ready; two hit the deck immediately, blood spurting from head wounds, no time even to scream. Octavia held back in the shadows. Outside she was sad to see the general hysteria of her own squad's reaction repeated across the camp. Dozens of half-dressed and hastily armed young zealots raced back and forth, anxious to shoot at something, anything, but unable to find a target; they shot into the air anyway, as if whatever it was would be scared by the noise. There were two slight indentations in the march-hardened sand near the centre of the quad, the puffs of smoke above them already dissipating. The machine-gun fire had come from the surrounding hills. Then, above the screams, she heard the unmistakable clatter of a helicopter gunship.

It appeared suddenly over the brow of the hill.

Outside they saw it too. And they yelled, and screamed and hurled abuse and pointed and fired and hurled some more abuse when they saw the American flag on its side. They weren't scared at all: what fools the Americans were to send one gunship against them.

Octavia shook her head. The Americans would *never* send one gunship; it was either piloted by some foolhardy nut well ahead of the main attack force, or it was there to lure them out into the open. As if to prove her point, seven gunships roared into view across the other side of the camp.

Fuck, she thought. She stepped from the cover of the hut. 'Boys!' she barked. 'Get on your bikes! These guys mean business.'

'We'll fight every last . . .'

'Fuckin' move it! If you scatter, some of you'll make it! Move!'

They were up and running. To her left three of the huts suddenly disintegrated. She ducked to the ground as debris flashed around her. *Jesus*. She ran forward, pulling the grenade launcher up to her shoulder.

Through the confusion Mohammed Salameh came to her.

'I can't find him . . .' she said.

He shook his head. 'He must be outside camp. If he's outside, he's okay.'

Salameh pulled his own grenade launcher up onto his shoulder. They looked at each other; a little smile. She knew it would end, one day, and in a way she was glad that it would end here, together, not with a bullet in the back of the head on some lonely Irish road, or with a quiet march down a long corridor to a firing squad, but here in the desert, buying time for their comrades.

He fired first. He missed.

A second later she pulled the trigger, letting out a little yelp as one of the gunships burst into flames then exploded.

'You always were the better shot,' Salameh said.

She gave the briefest smile, then aimed again.

The US Marines tagged sixty bodies, roughly half killed in the camp itself, the others shot down as they tried to escape into the open desert where they'd encountered the troops who had lain camouflaged in the surrounding hills for the past four days.

Two walked up the line of dead terrorists. Near the end, one kicked at a boot. 'That's her,' he laughed. 'Even if we don't get a goddamn medal for this, at least we come out of it with an excellent porn video.'

The second rolled Octavia over with his boot. 'She was beautiful,' he said.

'Yeah, and great tits.'

The remains of the solitary downed gunship and its thirteen occupants would be lifted back to the deck of the USS *Leonard*, lying one hundred miles offshore. Medals would probably be given and full military honours bestowed, but it would be logged as an unfortunate accident and quickly forgotten about.

After the gunships departed: movement in the ruins.

He had been asleep in the Tamil Tigers' recently vacated hut when the attack had begun. The force of a direct hit on the hut next door had forced in its walls. He had heard *their* screams but did not himself make a sound, even though he knew he was injured; a broken arm at least, and somewhere the throb of hot blood. He tried to move but found himself trapped by the weight of the corrugated iron on his legs. The rest of his body was covered by army canvas. All he could do was lie there and listen to the sound of the massacre, and weep silently.

Then there was an eerie silence, which seemed to last for an eternity, but which he later thought was only minutes. It was broken by bullish, gloating American voices, laughter and the pitiful groans of his injured comrades. And then some more gunfire, and the groans ceased.

After a while the voices diminished and he heard the helicopter gunships depart.

It grew cold and he shivered. He did not think that help would come. Not here. Not even the Libyans. He worked at freeing himself, pushing up and down and across. He suddenly felt claustrophobic; he needed to see the sky. He changed the emphasis of his struggle from the corrugated iron to the mass of canvas pinning him down. Using his good arm he managed to loose a little square of the aging material, then sucked greedily at the night air.

Above him the stars: so beautiful. He had spent entire nights just staring at them.

There was a sudden groan and the corrugated iron shifted. He winced but remained silent, fearful that whoever was rooting through the wreckage wouldn't take kindly to discovering a survivor. But there was no further movement, no furtive sounds; the wreckage of the hut had shifted of its own accord, or perhaps his own struggles against imprisonment had started something long before and were only now bearing fruit. Whatever, he could now move his legs. Gradually, an inch at a time, he was able to push himself backwards, up into the canvas, and from there his head, then his upper body, broken arm, then legs forced their way through into freedom – and the scene of the massacre.

His arm was hurting now; he examined his leg.

There was a long tear along his khaki trousers and a black scab had formed along his calf. He stood, stretched, and then began to check the remains of the camp. Thankfully, it was all somehow less horrific than he had feared: the sounds of the massacre had forced all sorts of bloody pictures into his mind, but the reality was that there were some smoking ruins and a long line of bodies. Nothing moved, nothing threatened. It was cold. It was dead.

He found an assault rifle lying in the sand. He picked it up, checked that it was loaded, then dusted it down.

He walked along the line of bodies, recognising faces, uniforms, boots; some he had known well, many had only arrived in the last few days. Near the end he stopped where he had hoped not to stop at all, lowered his head and said a quiet prayer. Octavia Maguire lay with her eyes open. He hoped her final sight had not been of the body that lay exploded behind her. He hoped they had looked at each other, kissed and expressed love before the end.

He stepped forward and gently closed Octavia's eyes. He put his fingers to his lips, kissed them, then put them to hers. He would have done the same for Salameh if he could have found a lip, even a face. He stood silently over them for a few moments, then turned away.

Mohammed Maguire Jr, aged ten, put his gun over his shoulder and walked into the desert.

2

He is a tattered little soul, walking mostly by night, sleeping where he falls or when he has the strength to dig himself into the sand. He wears his green army uniform, the one his mother made for him, the cap, black boots. When he rests he is careful to protect his rifle from the sand. Several times he is caught unawares by the *ghibli*, the blast-furnace desert wind that races and burns across the sand; he cries in pain, but the tears are dry before they can fall. As well as the gun he carries with him a one-litre bottle of water and one family bag of Opal Fruits, which he keeps inside the bottle of water. By noon on the second day both are boiled in the 120-degree heat.

He does not think of dying. That is not the way he has been taught. His father was a survivor. So was his mother. Although they are both dead now. He remembers what he ignored then, what his father told him: that we are all going to die, there is no escape, that it is the manner of your living that is important.

The sun dips and he rouses himself. His arm aches still, but no longer seems broken. He sits on the desert floor, still as the night, and waits. Forty minutes pass and nothing, then some slight movement and his good hand shoots out and he has it. A gerbil.

He thinks Rice Krispies. Snap as he breaks its spine. Crackle as he pounds the bones and pops the pulp into his mouth. He will survive.

But he shouldn't. Here is where the hottest shade temperature ever known – 136.4 degrees – was recorded. Mo walks through the exact spot. It is night, he's freezing.

Libya, but they weren't taught about Libya. The struggle was about the wider world. About freedom, and rights, and the evils of capitalism and Jews and English men and their colonialism and Americans and their domination. Libya is just their desert home and the Colonel is the benevolent leader nobody really trusts.

Mo walks east towards Egypt and he will keep walking until he gets there. His land is Ireland and you can walk to any part of it in a few days. He does not appreciate the sheer size of this country. He knows it is big, but not that it is bigger than all of Western Europe, and most of it desert. A ten-year-old's perspective on big is different. But he will not falter.

He walks and he walks and he walks and he knows that the blood is drying in his veins. Death is marching behind him. He must not stop.

On the fourth day a band of outcast Bedouin nomads keeping watch over a poisoned well two hundred miles south of Elgizira come across a dried-up little man dry-vomiting in the sand. They are scavengers by necessity and they make regular and occasionally lucrative trips to the well. This time the pickings are slim but not unuseful – a rifle and small boots. They will slit his throat rather than seek help for him; pity is a short word in more plentiful lands but a long haul in this box of sand. Then the boy gives one great heave; they cackle as the emaciated little body tortures itself, but as he rolls deliriously in the sand, unaware even that they are there, his cap comes off and instead of the black hair of the Arab there is the blond hair of the West. They stop laughing. They search him more thoroughly and discover a passport hidden in the lining of his jacket.

For three days he remains delirious. They give him water, bathe him, pray over him. He lies in a bed that is dragged across the sand by two of the three camels owned by these Bedouin. The third camel is ridden by Mohammed Abu Al-Asad Al-Alem, half blind and sixty-five. Two of his brothers walk at either side of him. Behind their brother's camel is another bed loaded with the scraps of metal, plastic containers and unexploded shells they have scavenged from the desert. Behind the sick child's camels, watching for thieves who would steal from thieves, walk two cousins.

When he wakes to the real world Mo is lying beside a weak fire. It is night-time and it is cold and there are dark figures hugging plastic plates of a foul-smelling substance. He lies still, as he has been trained to do, and listens; he understands little of what they say, and they say little. His body aches; the desert has sucked the life from it.

His body is racked by coughing, and they know now that he is awake. They greet him, and offer him a plate of the stew. He smiles and nods and gobbles it down and is sick again. They all laugh. An hour later he tries another plate, smaller, and eats it down, slower. This time it stays where it is. He sits up, dizzy still, and they give him water and then a dessert made of mint tea and hazelnuts.

Three tents are set up around the fire. After an hour of murmurs from which he can decipher nothing, one of the brothers leads Mo to the tent closest to the fire. There is an evil-smelling rug on the ground. The brother points at the rug, smiles, bows and leaves the tent. Mo still feels weak and does not hesitate to take the opportunity to sleep. His mother once told him, 'The Bedouin are no Dr Barnados,' so he will remain on his guard, but he must build his strength while he can.

Some time later Abu Al-Asad enters the tent and kneels beside him. He pats Mo's hair and massages his back and says something he doesn't understand. Then he lies beside him and goes to sleep.

He plans to be up before the others, to steal some food, retrieve his gun and disappear again into the desert. But he sleeps late and is roused jointly by a shake from the old man and the accompanying bellow of an old camel being beaten with a stick. The old man smiles and speaks, then leads him outside where they eat a dry breakfast before mounting up and resuming their journey. Mo asks where they are going. They do not understand, but he works out from the sun that the direction is east, so he decides to risk another day with them. Mo rides up front on Abu Al-Asad's camel. From time to time the old man reaches forward and massages his shoulders. Walking at his side, the brothers look up at him. He doesn't like their eyes; they are narrow and rove over his face and body as if they are thinking of eating him. Throughout the day the brothers reach up morsels of food to him – dried meat or nuts – and he takes them without acknowledgement, repelled by their crooked yellow-toothed smiles and the way they grasp his hands as he takes the food.

He tells himself he must not judge them like this. His father would not have allowed it. But then his father was a proud and mighty warrior, and these appear to be crap Bedouin.

Towards evening an ill-humoured Libyan army patrol stops the little caravan and rifles dismissively through their cargo of scrap. Mo is wearing Bedouin clothes now, his uniform stowed in a bag of rags tied to one of the camels. As the Libyans approach, his hosts hurry to hide what little valuables they have in the nether regions of their camels, to which the camels object violently. His hosts hover defensively about Mo's camel; Abu Al-Asad performs his usual massage, but this time his long fingernails grind into his back and Mo has to bite his lip to stop himself crying out. The old man is nervous.

The soldiers agree to trade some army rations for the unexploded shells, then move on.

That night the Bedo are in good humour. The fire is larger than usual. They eat all of the army rations and Mo is happy to eat more than most. But he is not stupid. He supposes they are treating him well because he is a Westerner, and therefore of value to someone. They have his passport, so it will only be a matter of time before they find out who he is. He supposes they will cross into Egypt before seeking to trade him in.

He supposes wrong.

As the fire dies he is led to his tent by the brothers. There he changes out of his Bedouin dress and is given fresh clothes; they are white, pristine. He is confused. Perhaps they are nearer the border than he thought.

The remaining brothers and the two cousins

enter the tent. They form a circle and sit, with Mo in the centre. They offer him water. He refuses.

Then Abu Al-Asad enters the tent. He is also wearing white robes. He takes Mo by the shoulders and begins to massage him, then begins to sing softly. The others join in.

Mo doesn't like this much.

Then the old man removes Mo's robes and when Mo tries to resist he grips his legs and begins to kiss his white skin. Mo tries to push him away but the old man laughs and pulls his legs from under him, then flips him onto his stomach.

Then he violates him.

As Mo screams the others laugh and the old half-blind Arab grunts and kisses and dribbles and fucks.

When he is finished the old man rolls off and gets stiffly to his feet. Mo lies bleeding on the ground. Abu Al-Asad leaves the tent and the others take their turn.

He has never known such pain.

The next day he rides Al-Asad's camel, which

doesn't help much. He bleeds and he bleeds and he bleeds and he is semi-conscious. They tie him to the camel to make sure he doesn't fall off; they know he cannot run away. Not yet. When he does open his eyes he sees them leering at him.

Of course, they are not total barbarians. They give him several days to recover before they take him again.

And after that several more days, and by then he realises that their lust is slowly diminishing. He is to them what his father would have called 'an old hat now'. They do not bother with 'the circle', but instead pass him from tent to tent; always the old man first, then the brothers in order of age, and then the cousins. He knows if the camels were that way inclined they would have their chance as well.

He still lies beside Abu Al-Asad, but he barely sleeps. He watches. His eyes are young-healthy and well used to the dark. When the old man snores he snakes out from under his crooked arm and explores the tent at first, and then the rest of the camp. All of them sleep like drunkards, but none of them drink. They are too used to the bad-tempered snorts of their camels to bother checking on every noise during the night.

By the end of his third night of exploration he has discovered his rifle, his passport and a rusting bayonet.

He knows that this night he will be taken again. There is an eagerness that begins in the hot sun, the little pleasantries, the patting of the hands, the massaging of the shoulders, the offer of their little morsels of food. He smiles now, and they smile too.

Towards nightfall they cross into Egypt. He can tell this by their excited jabber, a lightening in their demeanour, and a big sign that says EGYPT. It is battered and British, left over from fifty years before he was born. He does not know how long before they reach Egypt's version of civilisation, but he thinks they will try to barter him as soon as possible because even they must know that what they have done to him is wrong, that they must get the best deal for him and disappear back into the desert.

So they will have one more good night with him.

The old man enters the tent. Mo is naked already and lying on the mat. The old man begins to stroke his back, kiss his hair. As he tries to mount him Mo turns, shakes his head, points at his own genitals, then points at the old man. He repeats the action twice, and at last the old man comprehends and laughs. The boy is too young for fucking, but why not let him explore?

Abu Al-Asad stretches on the rug and lets the naked boy climb on top.

He rests his head on his folded arms and yawns. The boy begins to massage the old man's shoulders and the old man smiles at the weak but relaxing movement; the boy has learnt well.

From beneath the rug Mo removes the bayonet.

And cuts Abu Al-Asad's fucking throat from ear to ear.

*   *   *

There is barely a noise: just a delightful gurgling.

When he is sure the bastard is dead Mo dresses in the Bedouin gear then leaves the tent and locates his rifle and passport. He has six bullets. He positions himself on the far side of the fire, then screams his father's name.

The brothers and cousins come hurrying from their tents in varying stages of undress.

Mo, kneeling, aiming through the flames, shoots two of them dead. One brother takes a bullet to the shoulder and falls to his knees. A cousin, shielded by his relatives, screams and runs into the desert. Mo rises and crosses to the wounded brother. He cuts his fucking throat as well.

For thirty minutes Mo roves the desert in the vicinity of the camp, seeking the missing cousin, but there is no trace of him.

When he returns to the camp the camels roar at him. He shoots two of them in the head. He takes the Bedo's rifles, their food and hauls himself on top of the remaining camel. He cloaks his face and says a prayer then continues his journey.

3

Truth be told, his is not the most arduous of jobs. He rises late, makes his way to the office, does some little paperwork, then lunches at the Sheraton. Occasionally he goes back to the office after that, but more often than not he sleeps it off in a comfy chair and then takes a taxi home to get ready for dinner. The Irish embassy in Cairo is not the busiest place in the world.

This is one of those rare days when Michael Calhoon does return to the office after lunch, but only so he can sip rum and peruse his newly arrived three-week-old copy of the *Cork Examiner* in peace without some servile wog disturbing him. There are four embassy staff, himself (the ambassador), two secretaries and the cultural attaché, and hardly a smattering of Arabic or Egyptian or whatever the hell the lingo is between them.

They want as little to do with the surrounding country as they can get away with. They know they are only here to perpetuate the myth that Ireland has some international standing. In truth the embassy receives a handful of visits a year from drunk or stranded Irish nationals, and perhaps half a dozen enquiries from Egyptians seeking visas. These visa requests are generally refused unless the Egyptians speak English. When they come into the compound speaking the Queen's English more perfectly than the Queen, the embassy staff respond in Irish.

Engrossed in his rum and society gossip, a world he hardly knows but nevertheless misses dearly, he does not at first hear the phone ringing. His office door opens and one of his secretaries, Maeve, the fat one, points at his phone. He rolls his eyes and picks it up and an anxious voice, English without the local twist, asks him what he is going to do about the boy.

'What boy?'

'*The* boy. Is it true what they're saying?'

'Excuse me, but who the hell is this?'

'David. David Mitterick. *The Times*. Is it true about the boy?'

'Have we met?'

'Yes. Twice.'

And he tells him some cack about a French embassy party and a New Year's Eve bash with the British that Calhoon frankly doesn't believe, but he's intrigued anyway so he says, 'Now what's all this about a boy?'

'The boy that came out of the desert!'

'What feckin' boy?' Calhoon shouts.

'Have you not been listening to the radio?'

'I don't listen to the local crap.'

'The World Service!'

'Nor mindless British propaganda.'

'God Almighty! You haven't heard about the Irish boy?'

'Now . . . now . . . you didn't say the Irish boy!

You didn't once say *Irish* boy. Of course. Yes, of course I've heard about the Irish boy. Of course. Uhum. What have you heard?'

'Nothing that hasn't already been on . . . listen, Mr Ambassador, I hate to rush you, but I need a comment. Need it fast. I've a deadline, y'know. Can you give me a comment?'

'Yes, of course. Uhm. We'll do everything in our power.'

'Uhuh . . .?'

'We'll do everything in our power. To help the boy.'

'We'll do everything in our power to help the boy. That's it?'

'Is that not enough?'

'No offence, but it's a bit lame. Seeing as who he is.'

'And who is he when he's at home?'

'You don't know?'

'Of course I know. But do you?'

'Okay. So it hasn't been confirmed officially. Can you confirm it?'

'Not at this stage.'

'Off the record?'

'Not even off the record. Not at this stage. The poor chap has to be protected.'

'Even if he's the illegitimate son of Ireland's most wanted terrorist?'

'Uh-hum,' says Calhoon. 'Illegitimate, is he? That changes things.'

'His father is Mohammed Salameh. The Statue of Liberty bomber.'

'The . . .'

'The FBI's public enemy number one.'

'Oh my good gracious.'

'Have you anything to add to your statement, Ambassador?'

'No, sir, the statement remains the same. We'll do everything in our power to assess the boy.'

'Assess?'

'Yes, sir, assess. Once we get access to him. The Egyptians, goddamn them, are being niggardly about allowing us access. Then we can assess him.'

'Can I quote you on that, Ambassador?'

'On what?'

'Niggardly.'

'Of course not. What the hell's your game, anyway? It's just a figure of speech.'

'I'm sorry, I—'

'Start calling the bastards niggardly, you'll have the wogs up in arms. What the hell do you think this is, eh? A game? This young pup has walked out of the desert and all you can do is try and start a race riot. Where the hell's your sense, man? I thought you were with *The Times*? It's the *New York Times*, isn't it?'

'No, sir, I . . .'

He puts the phone down. He finishes his rum. Reluctantly Michael Calhoon folds his paper. Then he summons his staff.

Together they sit and listen to the BBC World Service for some reference to the Irish boy.

Police headquarters is a chaotic mess. The little bastard is squirrelled down in the bowels somewhere, away from prying eyes. Not that the wogs would know what the hell a squirrel was.

Police Captain Ibn Saud leads him through the building, an anxious man with a face like Nasser and a stomach as wide as the Nile, or maybe not quite. He's been trained at Hendon Police College in England and his voice is an odd mix of native and bully-boy colonial copper. 'We have been calling the embassy all morning,' he says, 'but no reply. Bloody phones on the blink again!'

'Oh dear,' says Calhoon.

'We'd been hearing about something in the desert for a few days,' Saud shouts as he pushes his way through a seemingly endless tide of sweating policemen and nervous clerks, 'about a white boy walking out of the sand more dead than alive. And believe me, Mr Ambassador, nobody walks out of that desert.'

'Gosh,' says Calhoon, beginning to gag now as the smell of piss increases with each downward step. He knows all about Egyptian cells. He has seen *Midnight Express*. Granted, that was Turkey, but it's the same neck of the woods. Finally they reach the basement and a long, dank corridor with cells on either side. The stench is appalling.

Calhoon takes out a handkerchief and holds it to his nose.

Saud sees his discomfort. 'I'm sorry,' he says, 'this is not the best place for a child, but here he is safe for a little while – you know there are many who would wish to talk to him. Believe me, I have had calls all morning. Newspapers, television, radio, CIA, MI5, even Mossad, they're all interested in this boy. But no, I say, we do not have him. I call you, I say, This is an Irish boy, you look after him. It is the least I can do.'

'Very decent of you,' Calhoon says.

'Not at all. Great respect I have for the Irish!'

'As indeed we have for your people.'

'James Joyce! Guinness drink! George Bernard Shaw! Yes indeed!'

Calhoon nods semi-enthusiastically and wishes he could repay the compliment. Cleopatra? Moses? Tutankhamen?

Saud stops at the end of the corridor, before the darkest and dankest-looking cell, then waves Calhoon forward. They peer through the small barred opening in the steel door.

'So young,' Saud says.

All Calhoon can see is a little bundle of rags

with a vaguely human shape. Hunched. There is a bed, table and two chairs, but the bundle sits on the floor, slowly rocking.

Calhoon shakes his head slowly. For the moment he forgets the stench. 'Let me in then,' he says quietly, his voice suddenly small and sympathetic.

The boy. He has a name, Calhoon just has difficulty using it. A passport photo, an angelic little photo and a name to strike terror into law enforcement agencies the world over. *Mohammed Maguire.*

It might as well say *Devil Spawn* in brackets after it. *Mohammed Maguire (Devil Spawn).*

'Hey, kid, how're ya doin'?' he says, and immediately knows the levity is misplaced. The head moves slowly upwards. The face is thick with dirt and dust and sand. Only the eyes seem alive. Blue and piercing: eyes that have a story to tell. But Calhoon isn't sure he wants to know.

'Hey,' Calhoon says softly, 'it's okay. I'm here to make sure everything's okay.'

The boy stares at him.

'Is there anything I can get you?' and it's another

stupid bloody question because he just needs to take one look at the cell and its very nothingness to know that it isn't a question of anything, it's a question of *everything*.

The boy's voice is raspy, and at first Calhoon doesn't understand. The boy says it again. Then Calhoon laughs.

'Opal Fruits? God, I'm not sure you can get them in Cairo.'

'Opal Fruits,' the boy says again, softly.

'I'll do my very best.'

The boy looks to the floor.

'Do you want to tell me how you came to be in the desert, Mo . . . hammed.'

He shakes his head.

'Do you know where your mummy and daddy are?'

He nods his head.

'If you tell me where they are, I can call them. They'll come and get you.'

'They are dead.'

'Oh.'

There is a silence then between them. The boy's

eyes look back towards the cell door. Saud's face is not pressed against the bars as a policeman's would be, listening for information. Instead he lounges against the corridor's opposite wall, uninterested. The boy's eyes are not scared, but suspicious. Suddenly Calhoon curses himself for being stupid. *Of course*. He has not been brought here out of any regard for Ireland or concern for the child, but to extract information. The boy has refused to speak to them. Now the cell is bugged. The world's security services are listening in.

Calhoon smiles. They are wondering about Opal Fruits.

And what the code is.

He looks at Mohammed Maguire, and Mohammed Maguire looks back. The eyes. They could be those of a man of sixty. He knows what is going on. They are sharp and predatory. Cunning and wise. He is the son of two of the most celebrated terrorists of the modern era. He has walked out of one of the most inhospitable deserts in the world.

He is ten years old.

4

He's a star, but you wouldn't know it to look at him. He's back in civilian gear now, black trousers, yellow sweatshirt, his hair cut short and his face scrubbed. He looks like he's on his way to a mate's birthday party. Instead he's on a Dublin-bound jumbo, sitting in First Class with Ambassador Calhoon, who has taken personal responsibility for him.

Traffic between Cairo and Dublin has never been heavy, and if anything has dipped since the ambassador's feeble efforts at encouraging economic cooperation between the two countries. The plane is less than half full. Twenty-six of the passengers in the rear of the plane are journalists from British and Irish tabloid newspapers. Occasionally they make individual or group efforts to penetrate the sanctity of the First Class section, but they are routinely turned back by the security men employed by the film company that is purchasing the movie rights to the Mohammed Maguire story. The journalists have to make do with throwing ice cubes at Michael Price, of the *Sun*, which has paid a considerable sum for exclusive newspaper access to the boy, during occasional forays back into a less privileged world to canoodle with the young reporter from the *Express* with whom he has been having a long affair for several days. Although he trusts her implicitly, he does not wish to compromise their relationship by telling her anything that the boy has said, much to her disgust. This is not difficult. The boy has said nothing. This despite the best efforts of the reporter, of Ambassador Calhoon, and of Tom De Wolf of VistaVox International Pictures.

Mohammed Maguire

Mo has a window seat and is only vaguely aware of what is going on around him. Calhoon has mentioned vast sums of money to him, but thus far has not stumped up with the Opal Fruits. He talks money and percentages and taxes; Mo just nods and signs the pieces of paper Mr Calhoon puts in front of him.

'You ever see *Jaws*, kid?' Tom De Wolf asks. De Wolf has greased-back hair and a motorcycle jacket, a white shirt and silk tie and black winklepicker boots. Calhoon has told Mo that De Wolf has a personal fortune of three hundred million dollars.

Mo nods.

'What say we make a big movie like that together, eh? A big scary, eh? You like scary movies?'

Mo nods.

'You ever do any acting, kid? In school?' De Wolf turns to Calhoon. 'Whaddya think, Michael, *The Mohammed Maguire Story*, starring Mohammed Maguire? Whaddya say? Big, big movie. You know how many Oscars *Lawrence of Arabia* got? And that was three hours about an English fruit. This has everything – a good-looking kid, international terrorism, US Marines . . .'

'US Marines?' Michael Price says. 'What're you . . .?'

'Yes, Marines! God is good to us!'

'*What* Marines?'

'Hey, Michael, you're behind the times . . . President Keneally announced this morning that Marines had wiped out a terrorist camp in the Libyan desert.'

'You mean . . .?'

'Yeah – you can call off the hounds, the kid's parents really are dead meat!'

Calhoon looks to Mo, who's looking out of the window, picking out shapes in the clouds. 'Mo,' he says softly.

'It's okay,' Mo says without looking round.

'Did you see them die?' Price calls across the aisle.

'Please . . .' says Calhoon.

Price pulls a face at him, raises a hand, and rubs the thumb and fingers together: cash. Calhoon reddens and just a tiny little bit of him regrets taking the deal with the *Sun*. Price nods from Calhoon to the boy, Calhoon rolls his eyes, shifts in his seat and touches Mo's shoulder.

'Mo, can you remember seeing Marines at the camp?'

Mo nods.

'Did you see what happened to your parents?'

He nods his head again.

'What happened?'

Mo shrugs. He continues to stare into the clouds.

Price taps Calhoon's shoulder and signals for him to leave his seat. Calhoon stands up wearily and crosses the aisle.

'Listen here, Paddy,' Price hisses, 'we've paid good fucking money for this, so you better get the little prick talking.'

'I'm doing my best,' Calhoon says. 'He's been through a lot . . .'

'I don't give a fuck. Open his fucking mouth.'

Calhoon turns back to his seat, but De Wolf has taken it.

'Sorry about your folks, kid,' he's saying, 'but shit, life expectancy ain't great in my game either.

Whaddya think, who would play them on the big screen, eh? What about your old man? I was thinking Hoffman. Dustin Hoffman – you seen him? Shit,' he turns to Calhoon, 'is Hoffman a Jew? Can you have a Jew playing an Arab terrorist? Shit – they all got big noses. Shit – not like you're going to see his dick anyway, eh kid? You circumcised?'

Mo turns, shakes his head.

'So Hoffman, okay? He'll jump at it. Him or Pacino. Pacino's not a Jew, is he? Nah. He's no Jew. Hey, you see *The Godfather*, kid? Great movie. Great movie! Pacino, he's a star. He could be your father. What about your mom, kid, any thoughts?'

Calhoon sits on the opposite side of the aisle with his head in his hands. Price leaves for a tongue-mingling session with his woman in steerage. Calhoon takes a glass of champagne from the hostess.

De Wolf takes two, gives one to Mo, who sips tentatively at it. Maybe if the kid's drunk he'll get more talkative. 'What you want is that colleen from *The Quiet Man*. You see *The Quiet Man*? Great movie. Great movie! Whaddya call her . . . hey, Michael, whaddya call her? *The Quiet Man*'s wife.'

'Maureen O'Hara,' Calhoon says wearily.

'Maureen O'Hara! Great. Pity she's freaking seventy-six now or something. Is she dead? Whatever, someone like her. Lots of red hair.'

'She didn't have red hair,' Mo says quietly.

'Sure she did. Her and Ginger Rogers. Redheads, both a them.'

'My mother,' Mo says, 'had black hair.'

'Mo. Mo! This is Hollywood. Believe me, she had red hair!'

While they're somewhere over Europe, the story changes.

Sinn Fein, the political-yeah-sure wing of the Provisional IRA, proclaims Mohammed Maguire a hero of the Republican cause. He thus instantly becomes an enemy of the British press. The message flashes across the skies: get the dirt on this tiny terrorist.

Price reluctantly removes his tongue from the *Express* to accept the message from the air hostess;

this snippet of information he has no hesitation in passing along. Cheques made out to the boy are already being cancelled; there's not much can be done about the cash for the ambassador besides turning it into a scandal that will result in his immediate recall from Cairo, although the correct protocol for recalling someone from Cairo who is already close to landing in Dublin has not yet been established by the Irish government. In the end they will fly him back to Cairo in order to recall him.

Price slips back into First. Calhoon is asleep. The film prick is trying to convince one of the hostesses to give him a blowjob in exchange for an audition for his next movie, and the little Irish bastard is drunk on champagne.

'So,' Price says, sidling in beside him, 'must have been pretty tough having two of the world's biggest murderers for parents.'

Something jolts Calhoon awake and for a moment he thinks the plane is falling out of the sky, that they're all about to die a horrible death; he has already crossed himself when he realises that something has struck his feet. When he looks down he sees that it is the reporter's head, and that there is an ugly red weal already forming along his brow. His eyes are open but unfocused, his breathing is laboured: he's trying to say something but nothing will come. He reaches up, paws at Calhoon's knee. Confused, Calhoon looks across the aisle. Mo is still in his seat, looking out the window . . . the film producer has disappeared . . .

'Mo . . .?'

Then he sees that Mo is trying to mask some heavy breathing. He glares across at him. 'Did you . . .?'

There is the faintest of smiles on the boy's lips.

Calhoon looks down at the reporter. 'What happened?' he asks. 'Are you having a stroke . . .?'

'He . . . he . . .' the reporter rasps, his finger jabbing back across the aisle, but he can't get any further.

No one has told Michael Calhoon anything about Sinn Fein. He half expects the president to be waiting on the tarmac at Dublin airport. He will lead the boy off the plane, Calhoon will shake the president's hand and eschew false modesty at his contribution to the creation of this modern Irish legend.

However this is not a good time for the Irish government to be promoting any son of an IRA vixen. As an emerging world force – it has a consulate in Cairo – the government has long been trying to repair fences (often quite literally) with the British. Terrorists on the run have been passed back across the border and it has cut back on its secret but widely known habit of providing guns but not bullets for the IRA. No, this is definitely not the time to be doing any public relations work on behalf of the Irish Republican Army. Yes, the boy has an Irish passport, but any official joy at his amazing survival against all odds will be tempered by condemnation of the very fact that a child was taken to a terrorist training camp at all, and, while applauding his great courage, the government can't help but feel that he would have been much better off polishing the silver in his local chapel.

5

There was some delay while they waited for an ambulance to arrive. Then the *Sun* reporter was carried off on a stretcher. The waiting reporters and photographers, believing that this was the desert-ravaged junior terrorist being rushed to hospital, took off in pursuit of the ambulance, leaving Calhoon and Mo to disembark alone, well ahead of the press remaining on the plane and before Tom De Wolf could be roused from his cocaine-induced coma by the film company security guards.

Calhoon was really, *really* pissed off. No presidential welcome. Not even a minor civil servant. Not even a car. Every taxi taken in the rain. Jostled, abused and assaulted as they stood getting soaked. Across the road there was the airport bus. He looked at it with growing fury. The Irish ambassador to Egypt was *not* getting public transport into the city.

And then he felt something, something strange, and he looked down. Mo had taken his hand and was looking up at him with little-boy-lost eyes. They were eyes to die for, or to be killed by. Calhoon felt suddenly paternal. 'Don't worry, son,' he said softly, squeezing the thin little paw, 'soon have you home.'

But where was home for Mohammed Maguire? His parents were dead. The poor little man had seen them die. Calhoon wanted to say something soothing, something reassuring. There was nothing at that moment that would be as soothing and reassuring as a ride. He suddenly caught a glimpse of a black cab and half yanked the arm out of his socket waving for it.

'Got it!' the ambassador yelled, dragging Mo forward as the taxi, ignoring a gesticulating nun, swerved into the kerb beside them. Calhoon opened the door and pushed Mo ahead of him into the back and then followed him in, slamming the door behind them. 'Well thank God for that!' he exclaimed and sat heavily back on the seat. 'Take me to civilisation!' he shouted, nudging Mo, who rewarded him with a grin.

There was a driver, ginger-haired and woolly-jumpered, who nodded back then turned the car out into the traffic, and there was someone else. The driver's mate. His navigator. The conductor. Calhoon didn't know or care. He was thinking about where to stage the press conference. He would not, of course, call it a press conference; he would need permission from his superiors for that; but just a few anonymous calls and the massed ranks of the press could 'surprise' him when he got home, get their interviews with himself and pictures of the boy nodding innocently, and there was nothing his superiors could do about it. It was *disgraceful* the way they'd been treated. Mo was a little hero, and he was being treated with at best apathy, at worst like a pariah. Calhoon tousled the boy's hair. There was no reaction. Mo was staring at the passenger seat, his face suddenly as pale and drained as when he'd first seen it in that dirty Egyptian dungeon. Calhoon followed his gaze; the passenger met his eyes. The face was lean and blackly bearded; his brown eyes were accentuated by tortoiseshell glasses, his complexion pasty. The passenger slid back the perspex panel dividing them and pushed his hand through the gap. Calhoon extended his own reluctantly.

'Michael Calhoon, isn't it?' the man said.

Calhoon nodded warily.

'Danny McAdam,' the man said.

Calhoon let go of the hand. '*Tar* McAdam?'

McAdam raised a solitary eyebrow, then burst into laughter.

Tar McAdam's ascendancy to the leadership of the Provisional IRA was swift and achieved with apt military efficiency.

The whole Republican movement was in disarray,

crying out for a new leader. The collapse of the much trumpeted Maze hunger strike on only its third day – *We were fuckin' starving* was the only excuse the prisoners could smuggle out – had dealt a body blow to the campaign and served only to gee up Unionist morale and further solidify British intransigence. The Provisional IRA's leadership was campaign-weary, too set in its ways. It was time for new blood, and inevitably that meant spilling some old blood.

Step forward Tar McAdam.

He was twenty-five; he had a degree in politics from Queen's University, Belfast, and if a degree in advanced bomb-making and massacre techniques had been available from Colonel Qaddafi he would have had that too. He never actually joined the Provos, preferring the autonomy of smaller, less strictly controlled groups; with the Provos there was too much history, and too many old men to keep happy. The groups he ran with were so small that he might almost have been described as a freelance, and his achievements were therefore all the more remarkable. He notched up fifteen kills in just three years, and only four of them had been innocent civilians. He also brokered the peace deal between the Belfast Association of Nationalists and the Official IRA, a deal that united the two small but important organisations under the umbrella name of the Banoffi. The Provos, for their part, kept a weakening eye on him, and acknowledged privately that he was turning into the most able military and political tactician of his generation. Naturally they wanted to kill him.

They planned the murder of Tar McAdam down to the finest detail, but had not planned on someone warning him. The tables were not only turned but sawed into tiny portions and buried on a landfill site in West Belfast, eight of the Provisional IRA's Army Council removed in one night in what became known as the Night of the Long Bananas. It was a revolution amongst the revolutionaries, and when the smoke cleared the Republican movement was dominated by an insurgent Banoffi with McAdam at their head.

A shiver ran through the land.

The campaign, military and political, was

rejuvenated. Not content with ruling by the gun, McAdam stood for office as well and was soon elected to the House of Commons. Naturally he did not want any truck with democracy and refused to take his seat. Instead he spoke at length about his plans for peace and privately threatened to kill anyone who stood in their way. As a man of peace he made sure that the bombings were confined only to police, army or civilian targets.

He also fell in love, and her name was Maguire.

'I'm not sure I should be in here with you,' Michael Calhoon said, his voice shaky, his brow damp. McAdam laughed again. 'In fact, if it's all the same to you, and no offence meant, but would you mind stopping the car? We can get another.'

'In this rain?'

'Our official car should be along any moment.'

'Come on, Michael, sit back, relax.' McAdam looked across at Mo, winked. 'How're you doin', son?' he asked.

Scowl was too short a word for the expression

on Mo's face. He sat back then huddled closer to Calhoon.

They had travelled for about a mile. Only now, when he rubbed at the misted windows, did Calhoon realise that they were not travelling in the direction of Dublin. At a roundabout he saw a green sign that said: *Belfast*.

Calhoon swallowed. 'What do you want?' he said weakly. 'I am a member of the government of the Irish Republic.'

'Not for long.'

'I am a personal friend of the president.'

'I'd keep that under your hat.'

'Am I being kidnapped?'

'No you're not.'

'What then?'

McAdam thumbed back. '*He* is.'

'You can't do that.'

'Watch me.'

'Why would you want to kidnap a poor defence-less boy?'

'Because he's poor and defenceless.'

'What're you going to do with him?'

'Exploit him ruthlessly.'

'You bastard!'

McAdam raised an eyebrow. Calhoon settled down.

'Y'know,' McAdam said, smiling at the boy, 'he's practically my stepson.'

'He's . . .?' Calhoon began, but was cut off by Mo snapping, 'I'm not your friggin' stepson!'

Tar McAdam laughed. 'I used to shag his ma.'

Mo leapt forward. McAdam speedily pulled the divider across so that Mo's tiny fist cracked harmlessly – for McAdam – on the cloudy perspex. McAdam was cackling. 'Exactly what we need!' he yelled. 'A little fighter! A bitta spirit!'

Mo slammed his other fist against the window. His pale face was red now, his eyes wide, his nostrils flared. Calhoon tried to pull him back into his seat but Mo pushed him angrily away. Calhoon was scared. Scared of McAdam, scared of this journey, but scared also of Mo and the look of violence in his little eyes.

*   *   *

By the time he left for his final Libyan camp Mo had barely spent more than three nights in the same house in the previous five years. It was the nature of the game his mother played, and, like any game, it came with its own specific rules. The constant packing was more to do with keeping the Protestant paramilitaries wrong-footed than avoiding detection by the British army. She had no doubt that if the army wanted to pick her up it could do so at any time. It did occasionally, usually at moments calculated to cause her the most embarrassment: when leaving Mo off to school, waiting for his eyes to be tested at the optician's, or while she was in bed with Tar McAdam. With the passing of the years the surveillance had become increasingly sophisticated; the army could bug every phone, intercept every letter, read her lips at two thousand yards, even if she spoke in Irish. She had once found an electronic bug in her bra. At that point Tar McAdam had insisted on her taking her bra off, and the rest was history. Being one of the most highly respected international terrorists of her day was one thing, but being lonely by night was another. She missed her Arab lover, and when they were together he was the only man for her, but this was Belfast and the nights were cold and damp and so usually were the makeshift beds. Like many upwardly thrusting women, she occasionally gave way to the temptation to enjoy an upward thrust herself. And who better, or worse, than Tar McAdam. He was young, attractive in an earthy sort of way, passionate, committed, funny and deranged. He was also the boss, which worried her.

Mo hated him from day one. And although they tried to deny it, giving him all the shite of the day about being good friends and Tar being his special uncle, he knew they were shagging.

He was used to sharing his mother's bed. She would always sing him to sleep, her voice soft and mellow, the old songs about protest and the men behind the wire and the martyrs to the cause, and sometimes stuff by The Carpenters. But now suddenly he was supposed to sleep on the couch downstairs waiting for some old bastard to switch the snooker off the TV and go to bed. Then he would lie in the darkness and hear bumps and grinds through the ceiling and know that they were doing it. Although *it* was always a bit vague in his mind.

He knew they were shaggin' because his mother had made him swear not to tell his father about Uncle Tar. And also because of the guilty way she came down in the mornings, her eyes puffed and avoiding his while they sat at the table and waited for last night's patriot to decide what they were having for breakfast, usually something fried and burnt and stinking. Usually he just saw the back of Tar McAdam, sneaking out before dawn to throw off the Brits, he said, though Mo'd heard he had a wife somewhere else in the city, in some other safe house.

It wasn't just the shagging either. Fights, too. Mo at the kitchen table, staring awkwardly into his stew, the patriot family listening with their pricked ears for every little snippet, while they blethered their lungs out upstairs. Always it was about the time they were due to go to Libya to see his father and enjoy summer camp.

*   *   *

About three miles from the border, just beyond Dundalk, their car drew to a halt at a Garda checkpoint. As the guard approached the driver's window Tar McAdam glanced back at Calhoon. 'You fuck this up, you're a fucking dead man, Calhoon.'

Calhoon swallowed.

The guard peered into the vehicle. He recognised McAdam immediately. Like most Irish police, he didn't carry a gun, but he'd been trained to use one: McAdam could tell by the way the policeman's hand went straight to his side, looking for a holster that wasn't there. Tar got a little rush, having that effect on people.

Tar spoke in Irish. The guard looked confused. 'We're on government business,' he repeated in English, 'hush-hush.' Then he thumbed back at Calhoon. 'Show them your papers,' Tar said.

Calhoon took out his papers and passed them forward. He avoided Mo's eyes as he did so. The guard looked at the papers, then reached for the radio clipped to his jacket. Tar said, 'Hush-hush.'

The guard hesitated, then his hand dropped away from his lapel.

In moments they were on their way again. Tar passed the papers back after a brief glance through them. 'So,' he said, grinning, 'how was Cairo?'

'Hot,' said Calhoon, unbuttoning the top button of his shirt.

This was going from bad to worse. Now he had okayed a dangerous terrorist through a police checkpoint. Any sort of contact between government officials and Sinn Fein had long been banned, and here he was going on a picnic with him. Calhoon's shirt was damp.

He was going to have to do something.

He had been kidnapped and was being taken north.

He was the victim.

But would it be looked at that way? *No.* He would be tainted. No matter how innocent he was, he would be tarred with the same brush as, well, Tar.

He took a deep breath. He had to do *something*.

He was an *ambassador*, for God's sake, he should be *ambassadorial*. He should negotiate with Tar McAdam. Come to an arrangement. Sign a fucking treaty. Whatever he did, he had to get out of the fucking car. He rubbed his brow. He licked his lips. He tried to come up with something to say, an opening gambit.

But there was nothing. If ever incisiveness and insight had been present, they had been dulled by his time in Cairo. He looked at the boy, staring morosely out of the other window. Mo had long ago let go of his hand. *I've let him down.* Slowly Calhoon's hand snaked across the seat towards Mo. A finger tapped lightly on Mo's left hand. Mo looked round. Calhoon roved his eyes towards the door handle, then back at Mo. Mo mouthed, 'What?' Calhoon's eyes darted back to the door handle, he momentarily let go of Mo's hand so that he could jab a thumb at the door, then grabbed the hand again. 'What?' Mo whispered.

Tar looked back at them.

'Not far to the border now,' Calhoon trumpeted.

Tar turned back.

They were approaching a roundabout. The traffic was heavy. They began to slow down. It was now or never. Escape. A dive for freedom. Disappear into the traffic. Tar McAdam would never give chase here in full view. It was their only chance.

They were almost at a stop when Calhoon grabbed Mo's hand, then rammed himself against the door with a shout of 'Let's go, Mo!'

His head clattered off the window. The door remained firmly closed. His shoulder jarred painfully out of joint. The driver braked. There were angry horn blasts from behind. Tar McAdam looked back and laughed while Michael Calhoon sat back and groaned. A tiny trickle of blood appeared from his scalp, dripping down onto his forehead, where it meandered lazily along between the furrows.

Tar McAdam got out of the car. Behind the traffic was starting to build up, but when the drivers saw who it was they soon stopped honking.

Tar stood by the window. Calhoon looked queasily up at him. Tar reached down and opened the door. 'Child lock,' he said.

Then he grabbed Calhoon and dragged him out by his lapels. Mo tried to hold on to him but wasn't strong enough. As he scrambled along the seat after the ambassador Tar turned and shoved him back in, then threw Calhoon to the ground.

'Thanks for your help,' Tar said as he stepped over the ambassador and slid into the back seat beside Mo. He slammed the door. The driver put his foot down and the vehicle shot out onto the roundabout.

Mo pulled himself upright, then turned to look back to where Calhoon, lying in the middle of the soaked road, had now curled himself into a ball.

'Right,' said Tar, his voice grim, 'it's time we had a little talk.'

6

The house was small and musty. There was an abundance of china in glass-fronted cabinets around the living room. A copy of his speech lay on the threadbare settee, and there were pictures of his mother on the walls. Mo stood looking at them as his granda heated a can of Campbell's soup in the kitchen. The pictures were not photographs exactly, but framed newspaper clippings, grainy shots of her firing volleys over coffins at IRA funerals, running with a gun across a ploughed field, being taken in for questioning by the RUC.

'Aye, she was a brave wee girl,' his granda said as he came into the room, carrying a tray with two bowls of tomato soup.

Mo turned from the pictures and sat down heavily on the settee, squashing the typewritten speech beneath him.

'You better watch that, son,' his granda said. 'Tar'll be . . .'

'I'm not reading it.'

His granda set the tray down on a poofy, then reached over and pulled the speech out from under Mo. He straightened it out. 'Of course you are. Tar wrote it special.'

'Not,' said Mo.

He set the speech down, then lifted a bowl and spoon and gave them to Mo on his knee.

'Tar says there'll be ten thousand people there.'

'I'm not reading it.'

'Eat your soup.' He took a spoonful. It was

lukewarm. 'Your mother was a hero,' his granda said. 'She sacrificed herself for Ireland. There's some nice crusty bread in the kitchen.'

'I know what she was. Do you want me to get you some?'

'No. I'm okay. Why won't you read it, son?'

'Why won't you? She's your daughter.'

'Because Tar wants you.'

'Tar can go to hell.'

His granda looked kindly at him. For several moments they supped noisily, then the old man put his spoon down and said, 'Do you want to tell me what happened to you in the desert?'

'No,' Mo said.

'Okay,' his granda said and picked up his spoon again. He dipped it into the soup, raised it, then hesitated. 'I can understand you being scared, in front of all those people.'

'I'm not scared of them.'

'What then?'

Mo shrugged.

'Mo, will you do it for me?'

Mo bit a lip.

'For your old granda?'

Mo shook his head.

'You know that Tar can make it very difficult for you if you don't read it.'

Mo nodded.

'And for me.'

He nodded again.

'Do you want that? Do you want Tar to send round the men with the hatchets to cut my legs off? At my age wooden legs don't grow on trees.'

Mo thought about that for a moment. Then he shook his head.

'Mo, I know you've lost your mammy, and it's hard, it's hard for me too. She was my only daughter. But she gave her life for Ireland, so that we might all one day live in peace in one big happy country. You know that, don't you?'

Mo nodded.

'So you'll read the speech?'

Mo shook his head.

The car came for him at four. It was a white Volvo with tinted windows. It was the same ginger-haired driver. He didn't know the girl who escorted him into the back seat and smiled at him like she was his big sister. She sat beside him. He wore his Sunday best. He had the speech in the inside pocket of his jacket. His granda got in the front beside the driver.

'Great day for it,' the driver said.

His granda nodded and looked nervously back at Mo, who looked nervously at the girl, who looked nervously out of the window. Her name was Mary Coyle, fifteen years old and recently promoted to the position of captain of the Fyffe, the junior girls' wing of the Banoffi. She wore a black blazer, a white shirt and a green tartan skirt. Her face was thin, pinched almost, her eyes blue and her complexion pale. Her hair was a very dark shade of red and she had a sprinkling of freckles beneath her eyes. She was the best accordion player on the Falls Road. Tar himself had asked her to escort Mo to the reading and she'd agreed enthusiastically. It was an honour. There was a lovebite on her neck, and when she turned from the window Mo was staring at it. She moved her hand to cover it.

'Stop it,' she hissed at him.

'Someone took a bite outta you,' Mo said.

'Piss off,' she said.

Mo looked out of the other window as the car pulled off the Falls and onto the West Link. They were heading for the City Hall. The driver said there were already about five thousand people waiting to hear Mo speak, although there were also some waiting to throw stones.

Mo gulped.

'Tar says you'll be great,' Mary said, remembering her responsibilities.

He ignored her. He stared out of the window. She reached across and nipped him.

'You better know your speech, you little desert rat,' she hissed.

Mo yelped and shouted, 'Fuck off!'

'Mo,' said his granda.

Mo nodded. He sucked his lips in bashfully then extended an apologetic hand to Mary. Before she could grasp it he flattened it out and gave her the fingers. He giggled as her eyes flared in fury, then she grabbed his fingers and bent them back as hard as she could. He yelped again and threw himself backwards to escape, his head cannoning off the window. The driver veered the car off to one side, fearing that someone had been shot.

'Mo!' his granda shouted. 'Settle down.'

They settled down.

Mo returned his gaze to the passing city. He rubbed the back of his head and tried to bend his fingers back into shape. They had come off the West Link now, and were moving towards the back of the City Hall. They passed people on the pavement carrying Tricolours. Irish music was blaring from loudspeakers somewhere ahead.

Mo thought his stomach was going to fall out of his pants.

After wishing with all his might never to have to face the desert again, after praying to God for salvation from the desert heat, he dearly wished he was back there.

Tar McAdam clapped his hands together when he saw Mo being led through the throng backstage. Led being the optimum word. Led, pulled, pushed.

He was only a wee lad and couldn't withstand the driver's tug, nor Mary's nips. One day, he swore, he would kill her.

'Ah now, wee man, c'mon through,' Tar said.

Mo had his first view of the crowd. Right enough, there were about five thousand. At the front. Behind them there were about ten thousand more. As Mo came into view a great cheer rose from the multitude, and his desert-browned face blanched. There were boos as well, from off on the right. He could see Orange banners.

Tar put his arm round him, hurried him forward. 'Look at this, Mo! Look at it!'

Mo looked at it.

'They're all here for your mother! They're paying tribute to a great freedom fighter! And not just her, Mo – you too! You survived! You walked out into that desert, you took on death itself. A thousand pale little Brits wouldn't have walked out of that desert, Mo, they would have given up on day one, but you took it on and you beat it! Your mother brought you up to be a fighter, and I'm going to make sure you fight for Ireland, and that Ireland fights for you. The Maguire family! Heroes from generation to generation!' He raised a fist, shook it at the crowd. 'C'mon, son, c'mon!'

As Tar McAdam led him forward the crowd roared. Mohammed Maguire, aged ten, shat in his pants, broke free and ran and ran and ran.

7

'*Master* Maguire? Stand up please.'

Mo stood. The rest of the class looked at him.
Fidgeted. They knew what was coming. This was
the fourth day in a row. His legs were black and
blue. He had bruises on his bruises. His granda
had said, 'What happened to your legs, son?'
and Mo had shrugged that shrug and said, 'Fell,' and
limped on.

His legs were shaking. He leant on the desk for
support, looked down. The desks were new this

term, but there were already thick black felt-tipped scrawls across them. *PIRA*, *Remember You're A Womble* and *Bum*.

'Master Maguire, I have asked you to write a composition about your experiences in the desert last summer. Have you written it?'

'No, Mister Simpson.'

Murmurings from the class.

'You know that Father McVeigh himself has asked you to write this, Mo. Not once, not twice, but three times.'

'Yes, Mister Simpson.'

'And that the great Tar McAdam asked Father McVeigh to ask you to write this, not once, not twice, but three times.'

'Yes, Mister Simpson.'

'And you still haven't done it?'

'No, Mister Simpson.'

'Would you like to tell me why?'

Mo shrugged. He looked at the desk again.

Mr Simpson came out from behind his desk. He was tall as a short giraffe and when he walked his legs splayed wide. Legend had it that he had been kicked so badly about the groin by the Brits that his penis had had to be amputated. He was known as No Cock Simpson about the school, even by the teachers, although not to his face.

Simpson stood before him now. 'Son,' he said softly, 'have you no sense?'

Mo shook his head.

'You're a stubborn little soul,' Simpson said. Then he stood back and said, 'Very well. We'll go and see Father McVeigh. Class, you have work to do.'

Simpson led Mo out of the class. They began to walk along the corridor, side by side, Simpson having to temper the width of his strides. Before they turned the corner to Father McVeigh's office, Simpson stopped him. 'Mo,' he said, 'you're being silly.'

Mo looked away. He took a deep breath, held it. He jammed his eyes shut then opened them. The tears were just beginning to form up like anxious troops waiting to go over the top. He would not let them come. Sooner or later, he reasoned, they would tire of hitting him, and then life would be okay again.

'All you have to do is write something. Make it up, Mo. For God's sake, they aren't going to know any different.'

Slowly Mo shook his head. Simpson shook his too. 'I don't know whether you're the bravest wee man I've ever met, or a stupid wee fool.'

'Stupid wee fool,' Mo said. Simpson laughed, ruffled his hair, then propelled him forward. 'I'm sorry,' he said after him.

No Cock was okay. It wasn't his fault. He lingered at the corner while Mo sat on one of the two chairs outside McVeigh's office. Another boy, Sandy O'Boyle, sat on the other.

Simpson tutted. 'What've you done now, Sandy?' he asked.

'Smokin',' said Sandy.

Simpson rolled his eyes. 'You'll never learn, son. Youse wait there now till Father McVeigh calls you, okay?'

They both nodded. Simpson gave Mo a last sympathetic look then returned to his class.

The corridor smelt of Dettol, like someone had boked on it and the Mister had cleaned it up.

Sandy was looking at him, gap-toothed and smiley.

'I don't know what you're fuckin' smilin' at,' Mo said.

'You,' said Sandy.

'You fuckin' stink,' said Mo. He did too. Of cigarettes.

'Fuck off,' said Sandy. Then added, 'I hear you got poked up the hole by a dirty Arab.'

'My father was a dirty Arab.'

'You got poked up the hole by your dad?'

'No.'

'Oh.'

They were silent for a little while. There was a smoked-glass door on the Father's office and once or twice they saw his gargantuan shadow pass across it. A phone would ring and he would bark a response then his voice would descend to a dull rumble. Maybe Father McVeigh was speaking to his granda, or the Boys' Home, or Tar McAdam.

'So,' said Sandy. 'Did you get poked up the hole by a dirty Arab?'

'No I bloody didn't.'

'Sean McTeer said you did.'

'How the fuck would he know?'

'His dad knows someone who knows someone who knows.'

'Sean McTeer is a fruit.'

'Takes one to know one.'

'Shut your face.'

'Shut your own face, boggy breath.'

'Fuck off.'

Then the shadow fell on the glass again and this time it opened. Father McVeigh looked from one to the other. He was huge and bald. He stuck a fat finger out at Mo. 'Inside,' he barked.

Mo took a deep breath and walked slowly forwards. The priest moved out of the doorway to allow him to enter, then stepped surprisingly briskly across the corridor and pulled Sandy up by his hair. 'You been smoking again, Sandy O'Boyle?'

Sandy nodded, though it hurt his head more.

'Didn't I tell you if I caught you again I'd crack your head off the wall?'

Sandy nodded, winced.

Father McVeigh cracked Sandy's head off the

wall. Stunned, Sandy staggered back, then dropped to the floor. He sat on his arse, his head revolving. 'Now get back to your class.'

The priest stepped back into his office and closed the door behind him.

Later Mo sat huddled in a corner of the playground. It was lunchtime. There had been some consoling comments from the boys in his class, but he hadn't been able to say much in reply and so they'd drifted off to play Gaelic on the gravelled half-empty car park. Then some of the older boys had come across and called him a cry-baby and pulled his hair and took his lunchbox and frisbeed his jam sandwiches through the air, and then one of them had grabbed his shoe and wrestled it off while he wailed and had thrown it over the wall into the girls' school, then they'd gone off, laughing.

He could hardly move for the pain of it. Father McVeigh had wielded the block of wood with even greater vigour than in the previous days. Before each lumpen thump he had asked Mo if he was going to write the composition about his experiences in the desert; each time Mo had shaken his head, then *whump*. There was still blood in his mouth from biting his tongue. The sound of eight hundred children playing jagged through his head like needles; his body ached and bled; he hated, he hated, he hated.

There was a gate just behind him that they were not supposed to use. It led into the girls' school and sometimes the smokers would congregate there but today the patrols had been stepped up and now there was just the rusty gate and the same cacophony of sound, only higher-pitched, coming from where the girls played their hopscotch and camogie. He had never been through the gate before. Boys in his class said there were boys, bigger boys, who'd gone through that gate and never come back. Torn to shreds. Sometimes just their ears were thrown back over the wall. It was said that No Cock kept an ear in his wallet and would flash it as a dire warning to anyone who ventured near the gate. In fact, one of them said that was how No Cock really came to have no cock. The girls.

Mo swallowed, peered through the bars. He could see his shoe. It was a brown brogue, just sitting, bored, a couple of feet out from the wall. The nearest girl was maybe twenty yards away. He could just leave it. He could hardly walk anyway; a missing shoe wasn't going to hinder him any. But then he thought of his granda, and how he'd explain it. There wasn't much money in the house, he knew that much, even less since he'd lost his job as a lollipop man outside the school. There was a new man there now, younger, a friend of Tar McAdam's, he said. So there was just the pension and that didn't go far; maybe there was enough for one shoe, but he wasn't sure if they sold them in singles, the way Sandy O'Boyle bought his cigarettes.

Mo edged through. The gate moved barely a millimetre; there was no rusting screech to give him away. He kept his back to the wall and took wide, sideways steps like a crab. One, two, three, four, then slowly he bent to retrieve it, his legs aching still; his fingers curled about the laces and he pulled it up and turned in the same motion and CRACK.

Something rattled his shins and he yelped and hopped on his one-shoed foot. A girl. Smaller than him. And CRACK. From behind, another girl, bigger, with a camogie stick in her hand, and then they were piling in from everywhere. He screamed and tried to hobble for the gate but there was a girl on his back, jabbing her fingers into his eyes and another had her hand on his groin and was punching him and then he was on the ground and they were raining wooden and fleshy blows upon him. He curled himself up as best he could, but the rain did not stop.

They were going to kill him.

It would be a relief, although he could have done without the pain.

Then, through the hysterical yells, he heard something, something loud and sharp and authoritative and the rain fell to a drizzle and then to a spit and suddenly there was just the angry murmur of war clouds and someone picked him up and he thought thank God for teacher, then blinked his glued shut eyes open.

It was Mary Coyle.

Someone aimed another kick at him and she spun on her heel, striking out with the palm of her hand. A bigger, fatter girl than Mary Coyle screamed and backed away, holding her nose. 'I'm fuckin' warning yees,' Mary Coyle yelled, her finger now moving around the half moon of attackers, 'leave him alone . . .'

'But Mary, he's a . . .'

'He's a hero . . . don't you know who this is? This is Mohammed Maguire.'

'You don't mean . . . Mister Shitey Pants?'

The girl got another slap in the chops. 'Now fuck off,' Mary shouted, and as she did the bells sounded on either side of the wall and the girls began to back away like unsatisfied vampires from the dawn.

Mo was sniffling, trying his best to stop the tears. Mary picked up the shoe where it had fallen and watched for a moment while he tried to pull it back onto his foot, but he was in such pain and distress that he couldn't get his foot into it. She took it back off him, sat him back against the wall, untied it, then slipped his foot in and began to tie it.

'You shouldn't really be in here, Mo,' Mary said.

He nodded. As she tied she saw that the bare inch of flesh between the bottom of his trousers and his rolled-down socks was bruised black. Her brow furrowed. The beating the girls had given him wouldn't show its results for a good while yet. She pushed the trouser leg up; he tried to push it down, but she slapped his hand out of the way. The bruises went all the way up his leg. She checked the other. It was the same. She sat back, looked at him.

'Mo,' she said softly, 'what has happened to you?'

He shook his head. The playground was mostly empty now. He would have to go, he would have to get to class. He tried to get up, but he'd no strength left. He moaned.

'Mo! Tell me, who did this?'

He shook his head.

'Was it the boys in your class?'

He shook his head.

'Please tell me, Mo. This isn't right.'

'Doesn't matter,' he said.

'Mo . . .'

'What do you care anyway? You're Tar McAdam's . . .'

'He asked me to look after you, Mo, and he never told me to stop. So I'll look after you.'

'But he doesn't . . .'

'Tell me about the bruises, Mo . . .'

'They'll heal . . .'

'Mo, if you don't tell me I'll march right in there and I'll tell Father McVeigh. Then he'll pull you right up in front of the whole school and make you tell him who did it. Make you point them out. You tell me, and I can sort it out.'

'Just leave me alone.'

'Right.' She stood up. 'I'm going to see Father Mc—'

'No!'

'It's the only . . .'

'No! For Jesus' sake . . .'

'I'm going . . .'

She began to move towards the gate. He threw

himself at her. He was only a wee lad, and she shrugged him off.

'Please!'

She stopped. 'So tell me.'

He looked at the ground. 'It *was* the Father.'

'What?'

'Father McVeigh done it.'

She smiled, then frowned. 'Mo . . .'

'He done it! He fuckin' done it.' He pushed himself back up onto his feet. 'Every fuckin' day this week!' The tears returned; he dropped his head, hiding his face, then tried to push past her back to his school, but she pushed him back, right up against the wall.

'Why?' she said simply. He tried to break free, but she held him tight. 'Why, Mo?'

'Because he wants me to write about what happened in the desert. And I won't.'

'Why won't you?'

'Because.'

'And he beats you because . . .'

'Yes.'

'The bastard,' said Mary. 'I'll tell Tar.'

'Tar knows.'

'You told him?'

Mo shook his head.

They looked at each other for several seconds. Mary shook her head. 'Oh,' she said. She let him go. She stood back against the wall, beside him, then let herself slip down till she was sitting on the ground. Mo slipped down beside her.

'I guess he doesn't like you very much,' she said.

'I guess not.'

'He thinks you let Ireland down.'

Mo shrugged.

'Mo, you can't go on getting beaten.'

'Yes I can.'

'You can't, Mo. You'll get septicaemia. Or something.'

He shrugged. They looked at the gravel.

'Mo?'

'What?'

'What would your mum have done?'

He shrugged. 'What difference . . .?'

'Mo. She was the greatest freedom fighter ever to come out of Ireland. You're her son. You walked out of the desert. You're made of the same stuff. You have to fight back.'

He shook his head. 'I can't,' he said sadly. 'I'm only ten.'

Now she looked like she would cry. She put her arm around him and hugged him to her, then kissed the top of his head. He snuggled into her. It felt warm and safe and lovely. She stroked the back of his neck and whispered, 'You won't always be ten, Mo.'

8

Three years passed. The beatings had stopped long ago because Mo had stopped going to school long ago. His granda didn't know any better; Mo just waited round the corner until the old man had gone out to the bookie's or the community centre and then slipped back into the house. The government's truancy inspectors rarely ventured into their part of town. No Cock Simpson called several times, but he never got in; Mo watched from behind the yellowed venetians, wanting to say hello, or at least fuck away off, but he remained quiet, then one day No Cock's tyres got slashed while he was knocking on Mo's door and after that he didn't come back. Father McVeigh wasn't going to waste time looking for him. Tar McAdam had other things on his mind.

There had been an escalation in violence. The Protestant paramilitaries, for so long a bigoted joke, had finally got themselves organised. For many years they'd just been gangsters, making a nice living out of it and occasionally slicing the throats of easy Catholic targets. If they tried something real, like planting a bomb, they invariably blew themselves up or were shopped to the police by an informer. When, for example, they attempted to kill Tar McAdam, they pumped sixty-three bullets into the black taxi carrying him to an election count and grazed his elbow. They were crap, and they knew it.

So they decided to get serious. Where the Banoffi and the Provos had benefited from the patronage – and, indeed, the madness – of Colonel Qaddafi, the Protestant paramilitaries like the Ulster

Volunteer Force, the Red Hand Commando and the Ulster Freedom Fighters – ostensibly one and the same but giving the impression of independence, mainly for tax purposes – turned to American benefactors for training and finance.

As Octavia Maguire had turned earnest young patriots into polished freedom fighters in the heat of the Sahara, so the white Anglo-Saxon Protestants of the Ku Klux Klan and White Armed Resistance had lent their assistance in turning cheeky little cut-throat gangsters into cheeky little cut-throat gangsters with the ability to kill and maim professionally. They also taught these educationally subnormal racketeers how to explain away their crimes by way of historical justification, sometimes using words with more than three syllables.

You can only teach stupid men so much, but for a while it jolted Tar McAdam out of his easy gypsy existence and turned his attention away from such frustrating little problems as the continued reticence of Mohammed Maguire.

So life became fun again, kind of. Freed from the twin constraints of education and ritual beatings, Mo blossomed, aided and abetted every step of the way by Sandy O'Boyle, expelled from school and now with a sixty-a-day habit to support. They divided their time between the amusement arcades on Castle Street and breaking into cars. They learnt to drive by trial and error.

On good days, when there were no security alerts about the city and they had had enough of sniffing petrol, they'd steal a car and drive all the way up the coast to Portrush. They took turns at the wheel, perched on top of cushions. Automatics were the best, you didn't need to reach any clutch pedal. They wore false moustaches to avoid second glances. A day on the beach, then break into one of the holiday homes, get drunk on sherry and cans of beer past their drink-by date, then sneak into a disco by the fire exit, stealing drinks, cadging fags, eyeing up cars outside. In the mornings they walked in the mist over Royal Portrush golf course gobbling magic mushrooms. It was an idyllic existence, and it couldn't last.

They'd broken into a Volvo parked outside Sean Graham's bookmakers on the Ormeau Road;

there'd been a couple of hundred cigarettes in the glove compartment and some cassette tapes that they bundled into their pockets. It was late on, but not as late as they thought, and suddenly the Hatfield bar a few yards down the street had disgorged its last drinkers.

Sandy hissed at him to move it, but Mo lingered, trying to wrest the cassette-radio from its base. Then Sandy was screaming in his ear, but Mo needed just one more second . . . and then it was too late; they were trapped inside the vehicle while a drunk searched for his keys. There was nothing to do but ram the doors open and run for it, but the drunk wasn't that drunk and brought Mo down with his foot. In the seconds before Mo scrambled away, laughing, into the darkness, the drunk got a good look at him and there was an instant of recognition.

Two days later the door of their little house burst open and four hooded men raced up the stairs and pulled Mo out of his bed. His granda came tearing in but they beat him over the head with baseball bats and he fell bleeding while Mo was dragged down the stairs wearing just his pyjamas and protesting his innocence of charges that had not yet been laid. He was bundled into a car and told to shut up, then taken to a drinking club on Beechmount Street off the Falls. When he got there Sandy O'Boyle was lying face down on the ground with a foot on his neck.

The first thing Sandy squeezed out was, 'I never gave them your name, Mo.' His face was thick with tears and his nose red with blood.

The other hoods took their hoods off. Mo only recognised the gingerhead driver who'd twice taken him places he didn't want to go. Another door opened and Tar McAdam entered, shaking his head. 'Mo,' he said, his moccasined footsteps barely audible on the wooden floor, 'what have you been up to?'

The hoods sat him roughly down on a chair. 'I didn't do nothing,' Mo said flatly.

'Ah now,' said Tar, 'there'd be witnesses said you did.'

'Aye, an oul' drunk,' Mo said, and then realised what a fucking eejit he was.

'If you'd been mine,' Tar said, up close now, circling, 'you'd have a bit more fucking sense. But you're fucking half marsh Arab, I suppose we can't expect much more.'

'Fuck you,' said Mo.

'On the contrary,' said Tar, 'fuck you,' and punched him in the face.

Mo went clattering back, his head bouncing off the floor. The other hoods laughed, Tar with them. Gingerhead came over and kicked Mo up the arse. When he turned his head Sandy was crying even more.

Tar flipped Mo over with his foot. 'Mo, son, there's enough fucking mayhem out there without wee skitters like you joining in.' Then he picked him up by the hair and pressed his face into Mo's, so close he could feel the brush hairs of his beard. 'We're fighting a war, Mo, and thus far you've done your level best not to get involved. And if you're not with us, you're against us, understand?'

Tar nodded Mo's head for him.

Mo spat in his face.

Tar threw him to the ground, then turned to Gingerhead and put his hand out. The hood gave him a gun; he stood over Mo, aimed at his head. Mo stared at him. He would not close his eyes. He would watch death coming for him.

Tar turned suddenly and shot Sandy O'Boyle twice in the legs.

9

'This is just fucking class,' Sandy said, both legs in plaster, like Laurel or Hardy.

Mo had brought him Lucozade. *Lucozade aids recovery*. He had stolen it from the Spar, that and a packet of Jaffa Cakes, but he'd wolfed the Jaffas down on the way over.

'Fucking class.'

He didn't mean it, of course. It was sarcasm. The lowest form of wit. Sandy thought sarcasm was fucking class, and he wasn't being sarcastic about it.

'You'll recover,' Mo said.

Sandy enquired about a can of petrol to sniff.

Mo said, 'Fuck off, I'm not bringing that into a fucking hospital.'

Sandy opened the Lucozade as quick as he could, checking to see if it was really four star. But it wasn't. It was Lucozade.

'Fucking class,' Sandy said again. He looked at his poor plastered knees. 'I wanted to be a footballer.'

'Sandy, you were crap at football.'

'But I wanted to be a footballer. I could have got better. Now I'll never know.'

'Aye.' Mo tutted. 'Look on the bright side. At least you're alive. And you'll probably get a claim out of it.'

'Aye, like I'll see that. The old guy'll get it and stick it on a three-legged horse. You know what he's like.'

'Has he been to see you?'

'Of course he has. Ate my grapes. Imagine doing that.'

'Imagine.'

'Don't be so fucking sarky. And he spat the seeds under the bed.'

Mo looked under the bed. He had. They looked like mouse droppings.

They sat silently for a while, listening to the coughing. Then Sandy said, 'I hate that cunt.'

'Your da's all right.'

'Not him. Tar McAdam.'

Mo nodded. 'Yeah.'

The next day he came back with another bottle, but on the third day he got caught by a store detective and even though he was able to do a runner he got picked up by the cops later on at home and was obliged to keep his head down for a couple of days. When he did get back to the hospital Sandy was gone.

Mo just gave a flat, 'Oh,' and said, 'That was quick.'

'Yes, it was,' said the nurse.

'What's he have, like, crutches or a wheelchair? I'll bet the lazy bugger got a wheelchair.'

The nurse looked at him. She raised a finger to her lip. Mo stared at her. She'd gone very

117

pale. 'I'm sorry, son. I . . .' She trailed off. Her eyes avoided his. 'Oh, God, son . . . nobody told you?'

'Nobody told me what?'

'The wee fella, Sandy . . . he . . .' Her eyes were red and her skin was white and her uniform was blue and the way her shoulders seemed to have crumpled down while she spoke she reminded him of a Union Jack at half mast, and he hated the Union Jack, although he'd been trained to love seeing it at half mast.

'Blood poisoning,' the nurse managed to say.

'Blood poisoning *what*?' Mo asked, his voice starting to crack.

'I'm sorry, love. It was on the news. Did you not see it on the news?'

'See *what* was on the news?'

'His funeral.'

There was a tiny metallic ting, the sound of a shilling dropping.

'Fucken wise up,' Mo said.

'I'm serious.'

'Fucken wise up,' Mo said again.

She looked at him sadly. 'I'm sorry. I thought they would have . . .'

'Fucken wise up!'

He turned and he ran. Somewhere along the corridor he heaved a Lucozade bottle through a window.

There was a little white cross. A little white cross and loads of flowers with the messages on the cards all run with the rain. It took him a while to track it down, and in the end he only found it because he found Sandy's dad standing on the far side of the graveyard, eating a sandwich, getting soaked.

'I've been here all day,' his dad said.

Mo had approached with some trepidation, thinking he might get blamed for Sandy getting shot in the first place. But there were no words of admonishment, just a great big sadness sitting on his shoulders like a cape.

'I only just found out,' Mo said.

'Do you want some?' Sandy's dad said, offering him a sandwich. Mo shook his head. It was a big thick doorstop, and the bread had been dyed red by the jam soaking through. 'I used to make them for him, every morning, for school. Only found out yesterday he hadn't been to school for two years. Funny the things you find out.'

Mo nodded.

'He was only fourteen,' his dad said.

Mo nodded again and said, 'I'm sorry.'

Later, at home, staring mindlessly at the TV, he came to a decision.

There had been words echoing in his head all day, old words from Mary, his friend Mary. *You walked out of the desert. You're made of the same stuff. You have to fight back.*

That's what she'd said. Mary. He hadn't seen her since that day. For a while he'd wondered what had happened to her. She was older, had probably left school now, was working in a factory somewhere or was married and watching the BBC, her revolutionary fervour as spent as the semen her flared-trousered wispy-moustached barman husband drunkenly left in her every night.

Mo shook himself.

You have to fight back.

He got up and went out into the back yard. It was cold, near freezing, and his breath made big misty puffs in the night air. He smoked an Embassy Regal, then began to dig around in the coal shed. He pulled quickly at the slack, his fingers working through the fine granules like a dog looking for a bone. It only took a few moments to find. His grandfather no longer had the strength, he said, to bring the coal in, so Mo had guessed it would be safe enough hiding it there. A black plastic bag. And within it a gun.

Sandy 'n' him had found it. Sandy, really. They'd been burgling a house out Malone way and had settled into their usual routine: Mo searching out the valuables and Sandy looking for somewhere to have a shite. Sandy always had a shite somewhere. In a handbag. In slippers. In the fruit basket. Nerves, Sandy had said, but he never used the toilet. Mo thought he probably just liked shitting in handbags and slippers. As the burglaries had moved on to progressively more exotic locations

– they'd started on the estates and ended up in the mansions – so had his quest for more exotic and inaccessible places to shit. On one of these, rifling through cupboards, squeezing himself into just the right position, he had upset a cardboard box, and out had tumbled the gun.

Small, old, and with six bullets.

Mo, who'd stayed clear of them, with reason, since his return from Libya, had taken it off Sandy despite his protestations about finders keepers. The last thing Sandy needed was a gun. Sandy was a head case.

He didn't put it back though. He took it home and cleaned it and made sure it was working. He hid it in the coal, but every so often he took it out and checked it. It was natural. He was his mother's son.

Even though things in the city had quieted down again, it took Mo several days to locate him. He still followed the old pattern, a different safe house every night, but Tar McAdam wasn't one for sitting in. He wanted to be amongst his people, so invariably of a night-time he could be spotted in one of the myriad illegal drinking dens to be found around the west of the city. They weren't much different to legal drinking dens, save that the Guinness was cheaper because it was stolen. There were tables and chairs and a TV up in the corner, and a little stage where someone usually got up half full and reeled off a folk song or two towards the end of the night, while someone else went round with a tin collecting for the political prisoners though everyone knew it went to buy guns and make bombs that resulted in more political prisoners, so in a way it was for the political prisoners, so they put in their money anyway, not that they would have dared say no. It was to places like this that Tar brought impressionable foreign journalists, Americans mostly, getting them drunk and enthusiastic for the cause, Tar sitting there with his pint and his pipe and his beard like a philosopher expounding on everything, a tweedy little Potato Plato surrounded by his cronies laughing or nodding at every insight. That's where he was when Mo found him, when Mo strolled past the security on the door because he knew the guy from selling stolen watches to him. He wasn't even searched.

He saw and smelt the pipe smoke before he saw Tar. He heard his raucous laugh before he saw his toothy grin.

He was sitting with a group of about five cronies and lots of pints. There was one other man, a journalist of course, with his notebook out and one of those armless jackets with twenty-one pockets more than anybody could possibly have use for. Tar was holding court, jabbing his pipe at the television screen up in the corner, and saying television was the only thing holding up a united Ireland.

'The only reason half this friggin' country thinks it's British is because the BBC beams its friggin' programmes into our livin' rooms every night. Every time we switch on, it's the news from England, the football from England, their cosy little sitcoms and travel shows and pop music, and they're not even real English people, they're little beings that exist only in the TV, they're friendly and witty and wise and we love them, but they're not English.'

It was crowded; the light was not good and what there was of it was smoky. Mo was able to move right up close, almost opposite Tar, moving the way his father had taught him to move through crowds, as if he were not there.

The American was trying to nod and grin and write at the same time.

'Anyone who's ever met a real Brit,' Tar continued, 'and I'm not just talking about soldiers, anyone who's ever met a real Brit hates them straight off. Cocky and snide of course, and so, so superior. That's why I really believe that the two communities here could get together, because if you forget for the moment about religion and politics, we all really do get on well together, same national character, same sense of humour.'

'But Mr McAdam, if the two communities . . .'

'Shhhh,' said Tar, nodding at the screen again, '*Coronation Street*'s coming on.'

And they burst into laughter: Tar, the journalist, even the hoods who should have been watching his back, and if not his back at least his front.

It was a few seconds before anyone noticed Mo standing in front of them, the gun drawn, and then it was Gingerhead, eyes wide with surprise, reaching for his gun, but too late. Tar McAdam was in his sights.

'This is for Sandy, you cunt,' Mo said, and started shooting.

The Ledge

They were cold now. Half an hour's procrastination had turned into six hours. They had talked some, but not much. There wasn't much to say. They were on a ledge and they wanted to die. But they'd have coffee first. The RUC inspector got them to agree to that. He was canny that way. It had taken him five hours to arrive; he'd been off on a course. He was their top negotiator, had been for fifteen years, degrees in psychology from several of the best universities, bald as a coot, whatever the hell a coot was. They, the ordinary uniformed police, told Mo and Mr Clarke and Santa all this in the run-up to his arrival, like it would impress them, and maybe it did because they still hadn't jumped. They were a little bit curious as to how he would do it, talk them in, and then he was there, sticking his shiny head out of the window and pleading earnestly, 'Please come in? C'mon in. Please? You don't want to die! C'mon! Please! Catch yourselves on!'

They shuffled away, unimpressed.

Inspector Campbell appeared at the next window along, a notebook in his hand. 'Now, lads, if I could just get your names, it would be very helpful.' He nodded at Mr Clarke. 'We'll start with you, eh?'

'What the hell difference does it make?' Mr Clarke cried, almost immediately adding, 'Clarke. Frank Clarke.'

'Address?'

'Forty-seven Blenheim Crescent. Belfast.'

Inspector Campbell nodded as he wrote. 'And reason for committing suicide?'

Mr Clarke's jaw dropped. 'Well,' he said.

'What the fuck's your game?' Mo snapped.

'Interfering git,' hissed Santa.

'Hush, lads,' said the inspector, 'I'll get to youse soon enough. Now, Frank, any thoughts on that?'

'I've . . . Well. I'm.'

'Okay,' said the inspector, 'I'll come back to you.'

He turned his attention to Santa. 'Now then, big fella, what's your name then?'

'Santa,' said Santa. 'Santa Claus. C-L-A-U-S.'

'Yes, very funny. But I scarcely think that this is a laughing matter. Now, let's try that again. Name, please, sir?'

'Santa,' said Santa. 'Santa Claus. F-U-C-K Y-O-U.'

Inspector Campbell's pen hovered above the notebook and his lower lip quivered. He looked up with genuinely sad eyes, or at least as genuinely sad as he could fake. 'Now, that's not very pleasant. I'm only trying to help.'

'Nobody asked you to help,' Mo spat. 'You just don't understand. We want to die.'

'Son,' began Inspector Campbell, his voice low and authoritative but in that certain police way also combative and condescending, 'if you wanted to die you'd have jumped by now. You know it, I know it. You came out here full of anger, resentment, but it takes just as brave a man to step back from the precipice as to . . .'

'Why don't you stick your pocket philosophy up your hole!' Mo bellowed.

'Aye,' said Santa, 'why don't you come out here and spout?'

Inspector Campbell rolled his eyes. 'Boys . . . *boys*!' he said, and climbed out onto the ledge.

'Don't come near us!' Mo shouted. 'We'll jump!'

'Don't be daft!' laughed the inspector. 'Just hold on to your horses.' He steadied himself against the wall. 'There now, nothing to be afraid . . .'

He looked down.

All those miles to the ground and the tiny people and the fire brigade with their woefully inadequate inflatable mattress and the hard concrete slabs waiting to smash his skull to smithereens.

Inspector Campbell froze. He could not move. Not an inch. Only his lips. 'Oh my God!' he whispered.

The breeze blew up a fraction and he felt himself falling forward, falling on wooden jointless legs.

Santa put out a hand to steady him.

'Don't touch me!' Inspector Campbell yelled.

It grew dark. There were spotlights on them now, and television camera crews jostling for the best shots. They were on the news. Inspector Campbell said, 'What am I going to do now? I'll be a laughing stock.'

'You were warned,' Mo said.

Beside the inspector, Santa sighed. 'Why do children hate me? All I try to do is make them happy, and all they do is howl.'

Mr Clarke tutted. 'It's the tacky bloody presents. And I choose them.' He swallowed. His throat was hangover dry. 'God,' he said, 'I'd do it all so differently.'

'My real name,' Santa said, out of the blue, 'is Raymond. But on the whole I think I prefer Santa.'

Inspector Campbell nodded gratefully. 'What are we calling you?' he said to Mo.

'Mo,' said Mo. 'Mo Maguire.'

'Mo?' said Mr Clarke. 'What's that short for? Maurice?'

'Mohammed,' said Mo, and waited.

It didn't take long. 'Mohammed?' said Santa.

'*Mohammed?*' said Mr Clarke.

'*Mohammed Maguire?*' said Inspector Campbell.

Mo nodded.

'*The* Mohammed Maguire.'

Mo nodded.

'The Statue of Liberty bombing Mohammed Maguire?' asked the inspector.

'No,' said Mo. 'That was my parents.'

'The Times Square massacre?' Santa asked.

'No,' Mo said, patiently. 'That was my parents.'

'The hunger strike Mohammed Maguire?' Mr Clarke enquired.

Mo shrugged.

'You're shrugging?' said Santa.

'You betrayed your people,' said Mr Clarke.

'He didn't betray *my* people,' said the inspector. 'He's a hero. He stood up to them.'

'Does any of this matter?' Mo snapped. 'I'm trying to kill myself here.'

'Yes, of course it matters,' Santa growled. 'If we all jump together we'll look like we're in cahoots.'

'Cahoots?' asked Mr Clarke.

'In it together,' clarified the inspector. 'I'd be proud to commit suicide with Mohammed Maguire after what he did, although I've no intention of committing suicide.'

'I didn't *do* anything,' Mo said.

'You did enough,' said Mr Clarke, 'to set back the cause by . . .'

'He brought peace,' the inspector cut in, then thought for a moment. 'Though admittedly it was preceded by some terrible violence.'

'Didn't you shoot Tar McAdam?' Mr Clarke asked.

'No I didn't,' Mo said. 'I missed him. I shot his chair and his pipe and his trousers. But no, I did not shoot Tar McAdam.'

'Should have,' said Inspector Campbell.

'I thought you went off to Hollywood,' said Santa.

'I did go off to Hollywood. Then I came back.'

'So what are you doing up here?'

'What the fuck do you think I'm doing up here?'

'I mean, what's driven you to this?' Santa nodded at the bear. They'd ignored him thus far. He'd just stood there, like a deaf relative at a funeral, contributing nothing, just swaying occasionally. 'I mean, it's not just about the bear, is it?'

'No,' Mo said wearily, 'it's not just about the bear.'

10

In a way it was inevitable. It was in the blood, and the blood was on the streets, and he'd lived on the streets for the past six months after busting out of the borstal while on remand for the third time.

Long Kesh. The Maze. *Prison.*

The judge had said it and Mo'd laughed like he was only joking, and then the smile had faded as they hauled him away with all the other killers and rebels, one and the same, and suddenly it wasn't the kid gloves and tuck shop of borstal, it was the H-Blocks. The judge had made his decision and he wouldn't go back on it, despite all and sundry telling him it would be a public relations nightmare to send such a little boy to such a big prison.

The bus took them away from Belfast, the motorway thick with mist, the guards looking at him with curiosity, the prisoners with glee. They knew a little about public relations as well.

Long Kesh was divided into two separate prisons, surrounded by seventeen-foot-high, two-mile-long concrete security walls and a dozen sentry boxes. The compound held special category prisoners, and they were to all intents and purposes prisoners of war. They lived in huts, had free association and the right to dig tunnels. However the British government decided this was not a good thing and decreed that in future all such Republican prisoners would be promoted to the rank of common criminals and held in normal cells. To this end eight new blocks were constructed at a cost of one million pounds each. Each wing, forming an H with its four uprights, contained twenty-five cells, a dining room, exercise yard and hobbies room. The central bar of the H was known with British reasoning as the Circle, and this held classrooms, offices for the warders, medical treatment rooms and stores. Other facilities, outside the blocks, included industrial workshops, an indoor sports hall, two all-weather sports pitches and a well-equipped hospital with dental surgery. There was snooker, basketball, vocational training from motor vehicle maintenance to horticulture, classes from art and music to Irish language and Braille. It was Butlitz. Half the prisoners in Europe would have killed to be there.

Mo was sullen in the van, sullen at the gates, sullen at the dark towers looming over him, sullen at the jovial greeting and sullen as they asked him to strip. He stood naked, aware of the difference between him and the other men; of the thick hair on their bodies, their smells, their stink of tobacco and sweat; he was clean and hairless and smelt of Vosene shampoo. He felt tiny without his boots, like any one of them could turn round and squash him into the ground.

They were giving out the uniforms. The prisoners accepted them with resignation. The fervour of their clenched-fist salutes to the judge had drained away and the reality of the years stretching away before them had begun to settle upon them just as the mist that still hugged the ground outside could not. Each dull-eyed man was asked his size and the nearest approximation in uniform was passed to him; each shook out the jacket and trousers and shook his head in disgust. They came to Mo.

'Size?'

Mo shrugged. The guard shrugged. He looked at the other guard. He shrugged back. They passed him a uniform. As the others had done, Mo shook it out before him, and then laughed. It was a man's uniform and he was still banging on the gates of puberty. It would be another five years before he could fill it.

'You must be joking me,' Mo said.

They shook their heads. Mo tried to pass the uniform back to them, but they wouldn't accept it. So he let it drop to the ground.

The guard picked it up and shoved it against his chest, forcing him back several steps. 'No fuckin' jokes in here, son, get it on ye,' he spat.

Mo threw it back.

The guard slapped him.

Mo lunged at him.

He was kicked back.

'Fuck sake,' said a prisoner, 'he's only a wee lad.'

That prisoner threw his uniform at a guard. The others followed suit. Then the prison officers surged forward, batons drawn. Heads were cracked. When it was over they were led naked to their cells, bleeding and bruising, leaving all of the uniforms lying on the ground behind them.

Soon word spread through the wings about Mo's defiant stand against the British government. By evening someone had written a song about it, and by morning not a soul in the H-Blocks was wearing a uniform. They sat defiantly hugged in their grey and scratchy prison blankets; even the old and infirm joined in, although in deference to their age and infirmity they were granted electric blanket status. Mo was a hero. He had a thin slice of a cut above his right eye and a missing tooth that you could only see, or not see, when he smiled, which he didn't, so that no one could see it or not see it anyway.

He was placed in a cell by himself. They were more innocent days, indeed, but not *that* innocent, and it had been a long time since any of them had shagged a woman. It was a well-appointed cell with bed, table, chair, reading light, bookcase and school books. But it was still a seven-foot-by-eight-foot concrete box and it was lonely.

The assistant prison chaplain, Father O'Driscoll, came to see him. He was tall and thin and his skin was as white as milk and his hair a sharp grey. He was known as Forktongue. He said, 'Son, son, isn't this a terrible state of affairs?'

Mo nodded, though he wasn't at all sure which terrible state of affairs Forktongue was referring to.

'Do you ever read the Bible, son?'

Mo shook his head. There was a heavy black

bible in the cell, sitting on the table, alone, like it was in solitary confinement itself.

'You don't say much, for someone who started a prison riot.'

Mo shrugged.

'Tell me, did you cause this riot as your reaction to the withdrawal of special category status, thus making the point that there is a distinction between paramilitary prisoners and common criminals, or is your protest bigger than that again, is it because of the British government's continued persecution of the Catholic minority in the North of Ireland or indeed over its entire imperial presence in Ireland?'

'The uniform was too big,' Mo said.

A careful smile appeared on the priest's face. 'You are a very smart young man,' he said, nodding slightly, 'to mask such cunning in so innocent a face. You will go far in the movement, I fear. Are you circumcised?'

'What?'

'Do you have a foreskin?'

'What?'

The priest reached for Mo's blanket. Mo scurried back across the bed and stuck his feet out in front of him. 'What the fuck are you playing at, you dirty bastard?' Mo shouted.

Forktongue laughed. 'I'm sorry. An understandable reaction. Forgive me. But do you have a foreskin and if so is it . . .?'

'What the fuck are you . . .?'

Forktongue raised a hand. 'I'm sorry. I get ahead of myself. You will be asked again.' He stood. 'You must be very careful,' he said, 'for they will try and exploit you. Both sides. If there is ever anything you wish to ask, if you aren't sure what is right, then come to me and I will do my best to advise you. No matter what you think of me now, I am your friend. I have been asked to look after you.'

Mo uncurled slowly. 'Who by?'

'I cannot say. But be warned. Tar McAdam wants to flush your head down the toilet.'

'What can I do?'

'Avoid toilets.' He smiled weakly. 'Watch out for him, Mo, he won't like this little show of strength.

You've only been here five minutes, and you've already united half the men behind you. So be careful.'

That night mournful songs rolled along the wings, ghostly Gaelic laments to fallen comrades that moved Mo to sleep. The only comrade Mo knew who had fallen, besides his mum, was Sandy, and he'd been felled by the very comrades these prisoners were busy eulogising. So fuck them. He slept and dreamt of the desert and the fun and the horror and when he woke in the morning his cell door was open and there was a guard, a big, beefy fellow he would come to know as Adair, grinning in at him.

'Slop out, you little shite,' he spat through his smile, and for a moment Mo didn't know what he was talking about. Then he nodded down at the po in the corner and Mo picked it up and took it to the doorway and joined the other prisoners on the blanket protest in pitching their poo into the shite trolley. The smell was disgusting, but nothing compared to that of the rancid Bedouin who'd once slabbered over him. The other prisoners smiled and winked at him and gave him the thumbs-up. After he gobbled down his breakfast of porridge, soggy toast and a glass of milk, Adair came and took him to see the Rat.

The Rat was the governor of the prison. Adair told him this as he walked him along the flickering fluorescent-lit corridor. Then, without warning, Adair suddenly whipped Mo's blanket off. Mo froze, naked, skinny, white, underdeveloped like Latvia, surprised by the attack, scared. Adair pushed him forward, laughing, his breath hot as Colman's mustard on his neck, and he tried to go forward but another guard stepped in front of him, blocking his way, and he was laughing too and Mo didn't understand what they wanted; he had a blinding flash of the desert and the Bedo but thought no, not here, not in the middle of a prison corridor with other guards lolling about the place, surely not here in . . . They made him stand still. He looked suddenly up at the ceiling, thinking for a moment that he was being forced under a shower, but no water came and he thought, *Gas?* But no, the guards weren't wearing masks . . . Suddenly there were boots kicking at his ankles, forcing them apart and hands gripping his arse. He looked down. There was a mirror on the floor. The guards were examining it.

'In case you've a rocket launcher up your hole,' one snapped.

Then the blanket was flung back at him and he was brought before the Rat.

He did indeed have the elongated features and yellowed teeth of a rat, but not the furry nose and long tail. His personal guards stood outside, confidently eyeing their domain. They felt safe here at work. It was outside that they felt queasy. Their wives felt queasy and their daughters and sons felt queasy. At any moment they could have their heads blown off because the comrades were sick of them being masters of their own domain. They were stupid. Because they were the masters they beat up the prisoners for little or no excuse, and they enjoyed it: they did not see the correlation between their behaviour on one side of the fence and their punishment on the other. They did not understand the dumb equation.

The Rat understood it, but it made no difference to the Rat because he was scheduled for execution anyway. It didn't matter what he did. He could bake them cakes and dance naked on their birthdays and he would still be executed, because he was the governor. But the prison officers, they were stupid. And grinning with it.

'Five minutes and already running a riot,' said the Rat, sitting on the edge of a table while Mo sat on a chair.

'That's what the Father said,' Mo said.

'Aye, well,' said the Rat. 'You know I didn't want you here in the first place. Your case went right to the very top after that fool judge sent you here. Up as far as Tin Knickers and still . . .' He saw Mo looking perplexed, then slapped his own head and said, 'I'm sorry. God. Sometimes I just slip into the language, I forget which one of us is really the prisoner. Your case went as high as the prime minister herself. She decreed that if you were old enough to carry a gun, you were old enough to carry the can.'

'I've never carried a gun,' Mo said innocently.

'Uhuh,' said the Rat. He sighed. 'If you continue this protest you'll double your time. You *are* aware that, whatever the judge sentenced you to, you only serve half of that time?'

'You mean he lied?'

'No. Well yes. But the same applies to everyone.'

'So he lies to everyone.'

'No. Well yes. Your sentence is automatically cut in half. But if you're on the blanket protest that half will be doubled.'

'So we serve our full sentence.'

'Yes. I think.' He looked pensively at Mo. 'There is a formula for working it out, but that's not my department.'

'How long are you serving?' Mo asked.

'Life,' said the Rat, regretfully. 'Someone lied to me too.'

'I'm glad we had this little chat,' Mo said, and stood up.

'Sit down,' the Rat said, 'and tell me what you want.'

Mo sat. 'A uniform that fits.'

'You're quite a little philosopher, aren't you?'

Mo shrugged.

'Whose writings influence you? Che Guevara is it? Or Connolly or Pearse?'

'I don't read.'

The Rat stroked his chin thoughtfully, then nodded. 'A man of action.'

The Rat pulled the chair out from the other side of the desk and sat heavily. He fished in his jacket pocket and produced a packet of cigarettes and offered one to Mo. Mo took it, leant forward to accept the light. The Rat cupped Mo's hand in his and looked into his eyes. Mo stared back. The Rat looked away.

'It's like a chess match, isn't it?' the Rat said.

'What is?'

'This. I am the Grand Master, I play three hundred games at a time, you are the earnest little boy who comes along and makes that lucky move, and suddenly I am defeated. Two hundred and ninety-nine victories, but what do they write about? The defeat by the plucky teenager. So what do you want, Mo? I can't let this spread.'

'A uniform that fits.'

The Rat sat back. 'When are you people going to learn to negotiate? Intransigence gets us nowhere. Mo, if you don't tell me, I can't help.'

'I told you.'

'What do you really want? I can't turn the clock back, Mo. We've spent all this money, eight million pounds, we've decorated, for Christ's sake. I can't take you back to Nissen huts, times have changed. Tin Knickers has decreed so.'

'All I want is a uniform that fits.'

'But a uniform that fits today is too constricting tomorrow. How can I ever win? I cannot lead the British troops out of Ulster, much as I would like to.'

'You would?'

'I would lead them out of Ulster and into the Republic. Take the fight to the enemy.' He tapped his fingers on the table. 'I cannot be seen to give ground on this, Mo Maguire. Are you refusing to wear prison uniform?'

Mo nodded. 'I'm refusing to wear *that* prison uniform.'

'Very well.' He stood. 'I had hoped it wouldn't come to this.' He shook his head. Twin points of yellowed teeth poked out from between his lips. 'I will inform the prime minister.'

11

They were a good bunch of lads, and he hated them. They were not that much older in real terms, not even in the depth of their terroristic experience. Most were in their early twenties, but physically they were daunting. Puberty is a difficult time for all teenagers, but particularly when you're banged up in prison with three hundred and fifty blanket-wearing men asking, 'Have yer balls dropped yet, son?' every morning with predictable monotony.

They meant no harm, but he hated them nevertheless.

The mornings were the worst. The Rat had decreed that the prisoners could only walk to the washrooms if they covered themselves with a towel. However he refused to provide them with a second towel for the return journey, thus forcing them to return clad in damp towels. There was some grumbling, but not much. It was only a short walk and better to have some protection when the screws took a boot at you as you passed.

Mo stood under the showers, petrified. Petrified of *the desert experience* and petrified by their very physicality. He willed hairs onto his balls and chest, he willed gruffness into his voice, and requested a disposable razor from the screws, but they just rubbed his soft chin and laughed and told him to come back in a few years and the rest of the comrades joined in the laughter. He stormed off naked, forgetting his towel in the rush to hide his tears. The jeers and laughter echoed after him then *came* after him, chasing him along the corridors; the screws, obligingly, gave him the run of the place so that his pain would continue. The only door they slammed in his face was his own, forcing him round and round again. They were just having fun, and he hated them for it.

He found an empty cell. He curled up naked on the bed, sobbing into the pillow. Then there was a voice in the doorway. 'Are you okay, son?'

'Fuck away off.'

'I would if you weren't on my bed.'

Mo looked up. He rubbed at his eyes. He sat up. He covered his balls, or lack of them, with his hands. The fella in the doorway smiled and threw him a towel. 'They're only rakin',' he said

'Aye,' said Mo, his voice cracked but a thousand years from breaking.

The fella laughed and came into the cell. He put out his hand. 'Bobby,' he said.

Mo nodded, put his own hand out. 'Mo, Mo . . .'

'I know who you are, Mo. I knew your mum. And your dad.'

'You were in . . .'

'Libya. Yeah. A few times. You were there too,

but you were very young. She was a fine woman. He was a great man.'

'And I have to spoil it all by crying.'

Bobby smiled. 'I've cried myself a few times, Mo, it's nothing to be ashamed of. Incidentally, how's your foreskin?'

Mo rocketed back on the bed. Bobby wasn't making a move. Mo relaxed, a little. 'What the fuck is this fascination with foreskins?' he demanded.

Bobby laughed out loud. 'I'm sorry. God, right enough, if you don't know you must think . . .' He laughed again, and removed his own towel. Mo looked away. He didn't need to have a reminder of his own unimpending puberty thrust in his face. Bobby was *doing* something to himself, and Mo couldn't help but bring his eyes back towards . . . ughh . . .

Bobby had his cock in his hands and was pulling the foreskin right back. Mo had messed about a bit himself but had never dreamt of just whipping it out in . . .

'Aaaah . . .'

And certainly he hoped when he came to try it would take a bit longer . . .

'Got it . . .'

Mo looked closer. From within the foreskin Bobby had produced a little rectangle of . . . *paper* . . . wrapped in . . . *cling film*? Bobby was laughing again as he saw the incredulity wash over Mo's face. 'What's the matter, Mo?' he giggled. 'You think we're all fruits?'

'I didn't know what to . . .'

Bobby removed the paper from its plastic wrapping and began to unfold it. When he was finished he held it up. 'Cigarette paper, Mo. Our chief method of communications between the wings. On a good day I can manage five or six. Big Jimmy McVeigh holds the record, forty-seven. Mind you, he didn't wank for a while after that.'

'Jesus. What sort of thing do you . . .?'

Bobby held the paper out to him. Mo held back. Bobby smiled again. 'You get used to it. Oh, political stuff, military stuff, gossip and Gaelic. Anything to get one over on the screws.'

'And they don't . . .?'

'Oh they suspect. That's why they have the mirrors for looking up our holes, but even then they don't get the half of it. The boys outside can get a message into us, we can get a reply out, and they can get a second message back in on the same day. It's magic. Everyone does it. Even those without the blessed foreskin. Up your hole with a big jam roll, so to speak. Mothers, daughters . . . in their bras, under their breasts, in their panties, in their tampons, in their vaginas . . . it's all to do with sleight of hand and not being overly modest. Look at it this way . . .'

Bobby spun on his heel and bent over, flicking away his towel to expose his arsehole. Mo looked away again, but this time came back quicker as Bobby began to probe his own orifice. In a few moments the sphered end of a small plastic tube had begun to emerge like a torpedo from a submarine. When the process was complete Bobby rubbed it against his towel, then held it up for Mo to see. It was what the doctors took their samples in, but it wasn't urine inside, it was . . .

'Crystals,' said Bobby. 'A crystal radio. These two wires . . .' Two wires trailed from the end of it. One he snagged on the window, the other he set on the heating pipes. 'One for an aerial, one to earth it, and . . . *voilà* . . .!'

It was low and it was garbled and distant and barely identifiable . . . but it was music.

Mo was suddenly laughing himself now. 'And they have no idea . . .'

'Not a fucking clue. Isn't it magic?'

There were footsteps in the corridor. In the moment it took Mo to sit back and pull the towel about him Bobby had whipped the radio back into its brown box and had begun to hum, but the footsteps receded and Mo stood up.

'I should get back . . .'

'Aye,' said Bobby, nodding. As Mo passed, Bobby stopped him with a hand on his shoulder. 'You did a very brave thing with the uniforms. And the boys appreciate it. Even if they do rake the life outta ye, when push comes to shove they're right there with you.'

Mo nodded slowly. 'I'm not really into all this . . .'

he began, then trailed off as an earnest light began to shine in Bobby's eyes.

'We understand each other, Mo, and the nature of the fight that lies before us. We know who the most successful terrorist of all time was, Mo, don't we? It wasn't Che or the Jackal or even your da. It was Gandhi. And he did nothing. He never lifted a gun or bombed a bus station. He just said no and let people react to that. And he changed the world, man, changed the world.'

'I don't want to change the world, Bobby, I just want a uniform that fits.'

'I know. And if we have to lay down all of our lives to get you one, we will.'

Mo nodded weakly and padded out into the corridor.

A week passed, and the showers in the morning did not get any easier. He grew to dread them. The boys had stopped raking him. Perhaps they realised that his distress was genuine. Possibly Bobby had a word. But he was convinced they were looking at him. Laughing at him. That at any moment they would push him to the ground and thrust the *Encyclopaedia Britannica* down his foreskin. He needed to be covered. He needed the protection of cloth. He asked for another towel.

'One towel, son,' said the screw.

'I need two,' said Mo. 'Preferably three.'

'One towel, son,' said the screw, and thumped him in the face. Mo reeled back, his gum split. Blood began to ooze between his shocked white fingers. The other screws were lining up, batons drawn already, facing the naked men in the showers.

'What the fuck was that for?' one of them, Francie, shouted.

'Free,' said the screw, and whacked him and another riot broke out.

They were placed in their cells. They smashed up the cells. Mo couldn't, because his hands weren't strong enough to break the furniture, but he made lots of furniture-smashing sounds.

They left the prisoners in their broken cells overnight then cleared out the debris in the morning.

Soon they had nothing but a mattress, a po and a bible. All but Mo, whose cell remained intact. Taking this as a good sign, the screws came to him first, four of them grouped smiling about the door. 'Wash, Mo?' Adair asked.

Mo said, 'I need two towels.'

'We only have one.'

'I need two.'

'Are you refusing to wash?'

Mo sat on his hands.

'Are you refusing to wash?'

Mo nodded.

'Prisoner refusing to wash. Make a note of that.'

They clanked the door shut and opened the next. The two prisoners in there shouted across in Gaelic, 'You washing, Mo?' except Mo didn't understand a word of Gaelic, at least nothing beyond the stock phrases. He grunted something.

It was enough, whatever it was.

'Then fuck you lot,' came the shout from the next cell, swiftly followed by the pound of leather on flesh.

That morning, nobody washed. Nor the next.

By the end of the first week they were humming, by the end of the second they were stinking. They had the most up-to-date and luxurious jail in Europe; it was only right and proper that by the end of the third week they should decide to cover the walls of their cells with shite.

It happened almost by accident. Since they had refused to wash, earning random beatings as a consequence, the best revenge they could muster, given that they had no other weapons with which to defend themselves, was to hurl their brimming pos at the advancing prison officers, or fling it out of the windows or pour it through the spyholes. The prison officers, being proper Protestant gentlemen and not accustomed to being covered in shite, retaliated by blocking the windows and the spyholes and refusing to allow the prisoners to slop out.

So the prisoners were locked in their cells with their buckets of shite. Bobby shouted through to him, 'Are y' all right, Mo?' and Mo said sure, and they got talking. At one point Mo said it reminded him of one of the survival techniques they'd been taught at summer camp.

'What, all this shite does?'

'Yeah. About putting shite on the walls so that when it dries out it provides extra insulation.'

For several minutes only silence came from the next cell. Mo, the only prisoner with a proper bed, lay back on it and stared at the roof. There were no shadows in this prison. No stars. When Bobby's voice came through it was quiet, respectful, almost in awe. 'Mo,' he said, 'I think that is a stunning piece of strategy.'

'What is?' Mo asked.

'Your plan.'

'What plan?'

'To put shite on the walls. It is the most disgusting, degrading, appalling and revolting thing I have ever heard. It will suit us down to the ground.'

'I was only telling you a story.'

'As Jesus told us his parables. You are a wonder, Mohammed Maguire. No wonder Tar McAdam wants you dead.'

'Tar McAdam wants me dead?'

'He does, but don't worry, this stuff will

probably get you first. Now get some sleep, I have some shouting to do.'

And he began to shout. In Gaelic. Most of the screws had gone home for the night, those few who remained didn't understand the language and couldn't fathom how it could be used for any sort of intelligent communication. Mo curled up in his blanket. He tried to imagine what life had been like before coming to the prison. It was only a few weeks ago, but already his memories of it were slipping away. This was his life, and somehow he knew it would also be his death.

12

It was a scene out of hell. On a bad night.

The shite, the long hair, the beards, the maggots, the stench, the pallid skin, the high-powered hoses, the screams, the shite, the beards, the maggots, the fetid skin, the infected eyes, the streaming sores, the beatings, the lice, the high-powered hoses, the Gaelic songs, the blast of the national anthem, the screams, the cries, the prayers, the stench, the thwack of leather on thick skin, the piss, the plops, the runs, the walks, the footprints, the stench, the horror, the screams, the lice, the maggots, the hell.

The Rat went off with nervous exhaustion. On his way home he stopped at traffic lights and a biker blew his head off. There were cheers through the H-Blocks and the screws waded in with batons and pulverised them, but not before they'd power-hosed the cells to make sure it was a good clean beating.

Through it all Mo felt inadequate. They had their long hair, their beards, they looked Biblical. His hair had barely grown an inch; there wasn't so much as bum fluff on his chin. He looked like a little boy. He had spent hours stretching his fore skin but it remained tight and unaccommodating to plastic-sheathed communications. He didn't care what they were protesting about, he just wanted to look part of it. To belong. He still had his nice room. The first time he had tried to smear his wall he came out in big red lumps and was rushed to the prison hospital, where they'd quickly estab-lished that he was not well enough to be returned for a beating. So they put him in bed and monitored him and prayed that his lumps would stay up so that they could give him a release on medical grounds, but the lumps sank back into his ghostly skin and they pronounced him fit to be returned to the cells on strict condition that he didn't try to cover his walls in his own shite or anyone else's, for that matter.

'Okay,' said Mo.

The stench was unbearable. Even with just a couple of days away from it he had forgotten how awful it was. He wanted to tell them to call it off, but they thought it was all his idea and every time they saw him they gave him the thumbs-up and told him what a wizard bloke he was. Top-ho and spiffing and wizard and other words they came up with to take the piss out of the Brits, even though there were no Brits, just Prods concerned for their heritage and Scots earning double time.

When he came back to his cell one day after a five-a-side football match – it was like having Moses and Rasputin and Billy Connolly on his team – there was a man sitting on his bed. He wore a black suit and a black tie and his shoes were the shiniest Mo had ever seen. His smile didn't seem to be fake, although his moustache did. He put out his hand and Mo shook it. 'I am the Mountain Climber. Perhaps you have heard of me?'

Mo shook his head. The Mountain Climber looked a little crestfallen. 'That's not your real name,' Mo said. Neither did he have mountain-climbing hands; Mo had climbed a mountain or two as part of his training. The Mountain Climber's hands were soft and pink and fleshy.

'No, of course not,' the Mountain Climber said, reclaiming his hand and examining it himself. He cleared his throat. 'It's a code name.'

'Oh.' Mo nodded for a moment, and then asked, 'Do I need one?'

'I don't think that will be necessary.' The Mountain Climber shifted uncomfortably. He had children of his own, seven of them, but he wasn't used to negotiating with them. 'Let me explain, Mohammed Maguire, why I am here. You may know that the prime minister has forbidden contact between the government and the IRA. The IRA similarly does not encourage contact between its members and members of the government, unless it involves explosives.' Mo nodded. 'However, despite these public protestations, there has always been contact. It is necessary. That contact has always been through a trusted intermediary. I am that trusted intermediary, the conduit between Tin Knickers and the IRA.'

Mo shrugged. 'If you say so.' Then he asked, 'Why *Mountain Climber*?'

'*Climb every mountain, ford every stream.*'

Mo looked blankly at him.

'*The Sound of Music.*' The Mountain Climber winked.

'You know about the radios?'

'What radios?'

'The music.'

'*The Sound of Music . . .*'

'*What* sound of music?'

The smile had slipped, and so had the moustache, a little. His eyes bored into Mo's. 'Are you taking the piss?'

'No one is taking the piss. That's the whole point.'

The Mountain Climber looked at the po. 'That's why I'm here.'

'To take the piss?'

'No! Yes! Metaphorically speaking. I've been given the power to broker a deal.'

'By who?'

'By everyone.'

'With who?'

'With you.'

'With me?'

'With you.'

'Why me?'

'Why not?'

Mo shrugged.

'Nobody wants this to continue,' the Mountain Climber said. 'But neither side can be seen to give way.'

Mo nodded. 'So,' he said, hoping it would lead somewhere.

'So, I've come to offer you a deal.'

'Me? Not us?'

'You. Not them.'

'Why me not them?'

'Because you lead, they follow, but where you lead, the powers that be don't want them to follow. IRA or Tin Knickers. They want to offer you a deal.'

'What sort of a deal?'

'Release on medical grounds. To a hospital. We'll say you had a mental breakdown. You may have to act a bit ga-ga for a while, but it'll get you out of here.'

'Into a loony bin?'

'Yes, but at least the walls won't be covered in excrement.'

Mo shook his head. 'I know about loony bins. Once you're in, you never get out. That's no deal at all.'

'Maximum of three months until the media interest dies down. Then we'll get you out of the country. Take you to America, give you a new identity. We have foster parents lined up already. Michael Calhoon, Ireland's ambassador to Hollywood, has agreed to take you.'

'I thought he was dead.'

'Only socially.'

'What about my grandfather?'

'He can visit. As long as you don't come home. If you come home, Tar McAdam will kill you.'

'He has agreed to this?'

'He suggested it. He doesn't want to kill you. The prime minister doesn't want to kill you either. It's the only time they've ever agreed about anything. They both think you're very dangerous.'

'Do you think I'm very dangerous?'

The Mountain Climber looked at him. At his innocent blue eyes and wan hairless cheek and grey jagged blanket pulled about him. 'Yes,' he said.

'Why?'

'Because they say so. I have no opinions of my own, it's why they use me.'

Mo nodded.

'So what will I tell them?' the Mountain Climber asked.

'All I want is a uniform that fits.'

'You know they can't do that.'

'I don't see what the problem is. Even if they just get someone to take the legs up a bit.'

The Mountain Climber smiled, despite himself. 'You say so little, but you mean so much. You are dangerous indeed, Mo Maguire. Will you accept the deal?'

'No.'

'Why not?'

'Because I'm not a loony.'

'But there's no suggest—'

'I've seen *One Flew Over The Cuckoo's Nest*.'

The Mountain Climber paused. 'But not *The Sound of Music*.' He stood up. He extended his hand again. 'I will convey your negative response to the powers that be. They will not be happy. Putting shit on the walls doesn't make good copy for either side.'

'Is that what all this is about, good copy?'

A shadow of disbelief crossed the Mountain Climber's face. He was discussing the media and its effects on Western civilisation with a teenager in a lice-ridden blanket. He pursed his lips. 'Of course it is,' he said and turned for the door.

'Well done, son,' Bobby said when they met in the queue for dinner. 'I heard about the Mountain Climber.'

'What did you hear?'

'That he wanted you to sell us down the river.'

'I would have. If he'd given me a uniform that fitted.'

Bobby glowed with pride. 'The British jackboot will never fit upon the fine-boned foot of Ireland.'

Mo nodded again and asked for peas.

13

'Mohammed Maguire, you have a visitor.'

Mo tutted. He slumped down on the bed. His grandfather was nothing if not conscientious about his visits. Once a week, when they were allowed, if the visits were not cancelled for some trifling reason or other, he would take the bus out from the Falls with all the other suffering relatives. And Mo would give his granda an awkward hug and they would sit opposite one another and talk about nothing: football and television and homework and what the other kids who weren't on the dirty protest were doing. 'Are you eating?' his grandpa would say, and produce a pie or ice cream or something sweet that had the indelible imprint of prison officer fingers upon it, enough to make him retch but not enough to stop him eating it, later, in the dark, when there were no shadows to haunt him.

It was the only time he wore his uniform. It was a prison rule that you could not have visitors unless you wore your uniform. The boys had had many meetings about it and finally decided that it was better to concede on this issue, meet the visitors, exchange the clingfilmed messages by whatever means they could. So Mo tripped and slipped his way through the corridors to the visiting area, and no wonder his granda said, 'Are you eating?' with the uniform hanging off him like a Biafran.

Mo was led by a sniggering guard – no reason, just sniggering – into the visitors' area and he looked about but there was no sign of . . .

A poke in the back from the guard and, 'Your cousin, last table, arsehole.'

And he looked and he saw and he didn't register at first. But she looked and she smiled and she waved, and Mary, his beautiful schoolyard saviour, was there. He hurried across. She flung her arms about him and fastened her mouth to his.

Surprised, his jaw dropped open. Which was just as well, as her tongue quickly filled the vacuum. For a moment he thought it had come loose in his mouth. That it had forced its way in and then committed suicide, but it felt too small, too dry . . . too *plastic*. A package. He recovered in time to close his jaw and lodge it in behind his back teeth and she let go of him and he rocked back on his heels, flushed, and he didn't know where to look.

The guard coughed, so they sat.

It went like that. Like it was a special language. Long Kesh Esperanto. Guard coughs, sit. Guard coughs, stand up. Guard coughs, less of the physical. Guard chokes, leave him to die, the fucker.

How long had it been? Four years. Four years at least. She seemed smaller. Or he was taller. But she was definitely older. She was a . . . *woman*. What must she be . . . eighteen, nineteen now?

She had been beautiful before, but he had not appreciated it; he had been into football and petrol. And now here she was before him, her gaze steady, her breath sweet, her . . .

'We're starting a campaign.'

'Who is?'

'I am.'

'For why?'

'To get you out.'

'That's good of you.'

'You'll die in here.'

Mo shrugged.

'It's disgusting. It's degrading. You're a hero. We've started a campaign.'

'We've . . .?'

'I've. "Free the Maguire One" hasn't much of a ring to it. But we'll come up with something better.'

'We?'

'I will. But the name doesn't matter. I phoned Amnesty International.'

'What did they say?'

'I don't know, the money ran out. But I argued persuasively for your release.'

'On what grounds?'

'That your trial was a sham. And a shame.'

'Oh,' said Mo.

'You were convicted on the basis of fabricated statements.'

Mo shrugged.

'Mo, why didn't you tell us?'

'Us?'

'Me. Why didn't you say?'

'Why didn't I say what?'

'That you couldn't read.'

Mo looked to the floor. At the expanse of uniform leg that hid his feet.

'I went to your school. I spoke to your teacher. From before your mother died. He said you couldn't read. Could barely write your own name.'

Mo shrugged.

'Why didn't you say?'

'I can read okay.'

'You were always on the run with your mum; you hardly went to school at all.'

'So what of it?'

'And when Tar asked you to read that speech

to all those people and you refused, it wasn't because you weren't a patriot, it was because you couldn't read, and wouldn't say.'

Mo shrugged.

'And if you can't read and you can't write, there's no way you can have made a statement admitting all those things . . .'

'All what things?'

'The murders, the robberies . . .'

'I never murdered no one . . .'

'Mo, don't you know what you're in here for?'

Mo shook his head wearily.

Mary shook hers too, so sadly. She reached a hand out to him and cupped his cheek. 'Oh, you poor dear lad, you just don't know what all this is about, do you?'

Mo shook his head.

The guard coughed.

Mo stood up.

'We'll have you out soon.'

'We . . .?' Mo began before he was marched out of the room.

*   *   *

Back in his cell, with the memory of her tongue, her real tongue, still fresh in his mind and the taste of it, the hint of Juicy Fruit and Tayto cheese and onion crisps, he lay on the bed. He eeked out the message from the gap in his back teeth, unsheathed it and studied the letters. She was right, of course, he couldn't read. Never mastered it. He could rattle off some of the better lines from Enid Blyton's Noddy books if he was pushed, but increasingly there was less demand for this than, say, in the early years of primary school.

The reading had all just seemed to stop. The summers in the desert, the winters roaming from safe house to safe house, there was never time for school, or if there was, there was never time for homework or for concentration. The important letters were IRA, RUC and UVF, not ABC.

He studied the tiny words on the creased cigarette paper. Usually he could make something out, pair a few of the letters together, make some sense, but this time no: and then he realised that it was probably Gaelic. He folded it into a tiny aeroplane and skimmed it across the cell. Then thought better of it and flattened it out again. Maybe it was important, maybe it was a love letter. He would ask Bobby, when they had a bit of privacy.

He lay back on the bed and thought of Mary. About her smile and her confidence and her enthusiasm. He had none of these things. Not even a smile. Or, yes, he had a smile, but he didn't use it. He kept it at the back of his mind, only to be taken out on special occasions, like a good coat, and even then it would need to be checked for mildew. He wondered what she thought of kissing him: had it been purely perfunctory, or had it started like that and rapidly become something else? The message had been passed successfully, but there was definitely a *linger*. Or was that just wishful thinking?

He dozed off. When he woke it was dark, but something was different.

His cell door was open, and he could faintly hear the sound of . . . *music*? It wasn't unknown, the screws teasing the rebels with Loyalist anthems, but this was different, this was . . . *pop*. He sat up, felt about for Mary's message, then slipped it into its plastic sheath and forced it into his arse. He hurried to the door and peered out. The corridor was also in darkness. The other cell doors lay open, with no sign of the occupants.

He padded along the corridor, hugging a blanket against him. Something was wrong. Something was . . . 'Is She Really Going Out With Him?' Joe Jackson. He loved that song, and it was playing at the end of the corridor.

He came to the association area. On a table at the side a candle was burning, smoking straight up, and in its weak light he began to make out the shape of his comrades. Twenty of them. In their blankets. With their wild Jesus beards and hair, dancing together in the candlelight. To Joe Jackson. And as he looked for the source of the music he saw that it came from different sides of the room. On one table, his blanket hitched up over his arse, knelt a comrade called Sean, the crystal set protruding from between his cheeks. Across the room from him, another one, Harry, knelt on another table, another crystal set sticking out of his arse. Earth and aerial wires led from both to radiators and windows.

Mo turned suddenly as someone snagged his arm. Bobby's bearded face loomed out of the gloom. 'Fuckin' cracker, eh?' he laughed. 'We got it in stereo. Are ye dancin'?'

Without waiting for a reply, Bobby pulled him into the middle of the floor and began to groove. Mo looked at him, embarrassed, for several long moments. He had been to discos before, with his mum, casing them for bombs, and a couple of times with Sandy when they were on the run with cars: they had always been loud, everyone talking at once, shouting above the music, clinking glasses, stiletto heels on wooden floors, girls, high-pitched laughter, shouts and threats and the DJ ranting mindlessly; but this was quiet, bare feet on cold floor, almost as if they were doing a silent mime of a noisy nightclub. Deaf-disco.

Bobby pulled his arm again. 'C'mon!' and hunched down and worked his arms like he was on the final straight of a fifteen hundred metres.

Mo hunched down too, moved his arms, shuffled his feet. 'I never danced before,' he whispered.

'Aye, and I'm fuckin' John Travolta.' Bobby

cackled. He thumbed across to where Francie was giving it everything. 'Look at fuckin' Olivia Neutron Bomb over there.'

Mo giggled. 'What's going on,' he whispered, 'where are all the . . .?'

'Strike. Two more of them got shot last night. *Shame*. They want better protection. Can't blame them.'

'And they've just left the cells open . . .'

'Yeah. Happens from time to time. There's a skeleton crew, but they're not bothering us. Still, we have to keep the radios up the old arses just in case they change their minds and decide to raid: they're too valuable to lose.' He leant forward and whispered in Mo's ear. 'Listen, mate, make sure you're not standing by the radios when ten o'clock comes round.'

'Why, what's the . . .?'

'Ten o'clock news, they'll need someone to retune the radios. Those wee fingers of yours, y' know . . .?'

Bobby cackled again. The song came to an end. The Who came on. 'The Kids Are All Right'. They stood arm in arm, yelling the chorus together. Then there was another shout and they were all yelling and clapping their hands as a comrade he knew as Patsy came through the door with a plastic jug in his hand. He began to pass it amongst the comrades. Each took a long guzzle, then peeled away, gasping, then laughing. Every time Mo went to reach for it it was moved out of his grasp.

Finally Bobby got hold of it, took a long drink, then held it out to him. 'If the wee bugger's old enough to be in here, he's old enough to get pished for Ireland,' he announced.

Mo grasped the jug, smelt it, but it smelt of nothing. So he drank it back.

What's the big . . .?

His tongue went numb.

His eyeballs began to revolve.

The hair that would not grow began to curl. If he took another drink he would have an Afro.

Mo staggered back on legs that were suddenly missing their muscles. He tried to speak, but nothing would come. And all to the sound of laughter and 'She's Got Bette Davis Eyes'.

Naturally, he had another mouthful as soon as he could, and then there was no problem with the dancing. He led it. He limbo-danced. He pogoed. He duck-walked. He yelled and he sang and he put his arms round his comrades and he pledged his soul to Ireland and the IRA and the Banoffi, though if anyone had asked him to enrol in the British army and take part in Bloody Sunday he would have agreed to that as well. He knew at one point that they were laughing at him. They cleared the dancefloor, standing in a circle, laughing and pointing and doubling up and holding their sides as he gyrated to something by Alvin Stardust, but he didn't care, this was the best night of his life. Maybe there was a purpose to all this, maybe they were all on the same side, maybe Ireland was worth fighting for, maybe his mother had sacrificed herself for a good reason, maybe he should have tried putting his hands up inside Mary's blouse, maybe that was what she really wanted, maybe that was why she had come so close, maybe that was the etiquette, she makes the first move, slipping the tongue, he makes the second, feeling the breasts, then it would be her turn, slipping her hand . . .

Wow! The room was starting to move. He reached out to hold onto something, but there was nothing, just his comrades, moving away, pushing him back, enjoying the show.

Stand still! He needed the support. The wall was there; he could see it beyond the candle, but it was an ocean of darkness away and he was beginning to flounder. The ground suddenly wasn't the ground, it was the ceiling. Why was the room spinning? How did they do that? Like a hamster wheel. He was getting nowhere. The music was suddenly louder, but muddier, it was . . . 'Rat Race' by the . . . by the . . . God he knew this, but the name wouldn't come . . . *the wall, must get to the wall . . . safety, sacrilege . . . no, not sacrilege*, what did he mean . . . *sacré . . . bleu . . . sacrilege, sacrilege . . . The Specials! . . . what was the fucking word . . . sacrilege . . . sacrilege . . . protection, protection, safety, sacrilege, sacrilege . . . c'mon, c'mon . . .* he was drowning, he was going under, he had to get to the wall, hang on to it, *seek protection, claim . . . sacrilege . . . claim . . . sanctuary!*

Fucking sanctuary! He shouted it out. He yelled, *'Sanctuary! Sanctuary!'* and affixed himself to the wall, but there was nowhere to hold on, no clefts, *clefts?* What did he mean, what did he . . . he was slipping; it was a sheer cliff and there were craggy rocks below with huge waves breaking . . . and there was a huge wave breaking up his throat. He let go of the wall, *freefalling*, no parachute, and thudded off the floor, then he vomited and someone was holding his head up out of it, pulling him up . . .

'No . . . no . . . leave me . . . don't touch . . .'

He threw again. And again. And they were laughing and dancing and . . .

'Just leave me alone . . . I'll be okay . . . I just . . .'

And he threw and he curled up, and then there was a familiar voice . . .

'Are ye all right, wee man?'

'I just want to . . .'

And then he remembered and his hand moved to his arse and he poked and he searched and he found the message. He passed it to Bobby.

'Read it to me, Bobby,' he whispered, 'I can't

read it at all, tell me she loves me, won't you, tell me she loves me?'

And the room began to spin again and he heard Bobby say, 'Of course she loves you,' and it began to darken, and he felt warm and sleep came upon him to the accompaniment of 'Bat Out of Hell'.

14

Fluorescent light.

Painful bloody fluorescent light. Footsteps. The tramp of warders' boots, each step a mini earthquake. He had his hands over his face, fingertips pressing into his forehead, trying to take away the pain, trying to find the thousand little ants burrowing into his skull, trying to prise them out and throw them away, but he couldn't find a single one. He could not swallow. His throat was so dry that camels had collapsed there from dehydration and were beginning to rot in the merciless sunlight.

There was movement at the door. He forced open an eye. Blinked against the shards of pain . . . Adair, a trolley, 'Breakfast, son.'

'Fuck off,' he managed, and buried his head further into the pillow. The trolley was wheeled away to the next cell; voices drifted across, but he could not grasp them; urgent voices.

Twenty minutes or twenty days passed and then the trolley was back at the door, but this time there were three screws and beside them, looking grave, the priest. What was his name . . .?

Mo groaned.

'Breakfast, Mohammed Maguire,' Adair snapped.

His whole body shuddered, heaved. 'No . . .'

The server looked to the guards, the guards looked to the priest.

'It's sausages . . . beans . . . scrambled eggs . . .'

'Oh Jesus,' said Mo.

'Or there's cornflakes or porridge . . . you can have them all, or any combination.'

They were being unusually generous, or cruel. He was going to be sick.

The priest said, 'Please, Mo.'

'I can't,' Mo said.

'Mo, just take something.'

'I can't.'

'Please, Mo, in the name of God.'

'Take it away! I'm not fucking eating it!'

He really was going to be sick. The room was starting to spin again.

The priest turned to the guards. 'Just hold on a wee minute.' They nodded warily. The priest came into the cell and knelt beside Mo's bed.

'Mo, please,' he said quietly. 'Eat something.'

Mo shook his head. He felt his brain *shift*. 'I can't,' he groaned.

'Mo, please. Don't let it be you. You're only a wee fella, you have your whole life ahead of you. Don't let it end like this.'

What was he talking about? It was a hangover. The worst hangover since the beginning of time, but still a hangover. Unless. *Unless*. The poteen. Whatever it was. If it was poisoned, if they were all dying . . .

'The others,' he croaked, 'are they . . . okay?'

'You know that they will support you, whatever you choose to do. But I appeal to you, Mo, it just isn't worth it.'

Mo whispered, 'I'm never drinking again.'

What little colour there was seemed to drain from the priest's face. 'Mo – please, no, don't say that. You *must* drink . . . without it you won't last a week . . . Mo, please!'

He jumped to his feet, he hurried to the door. 'Please . . . give me some water . . . yes, yes . . . thank you . . .'

He dashed back to Mo's side. 'Please, Mo,' he said urgently, 'you must take water . . .'

Mo blinked at him, then moved his head up slightly, spin, spin, spin, smiled weakly and accepted the tumbler. He took several small sips then handed it back to the priest, who nodded gratefully. Mo put his head back on the pillow.

'Enough,' he said.

'Mo,' the priest said, 'I urge you to reconsider.'

'I can't,' Mo said. 'I'm sick.'

'We are all sick of this.' The priest sucked one

of his lips, his own lips, into his mouth. His face was an odd mix of despair and awe. He made the sign of the cross. 'I think you are the bravest man ever walked this planet, Mohammed Maguire.'

Mo managed to nod. *What the fuck is he talking about? Can't he see I'm dying here? Just leave me alone. Let me sleep. I'll be fine.*

The priest stood up, gazed down on the half-conscious boy, shook his head, then crossed to the door. 'I've done my best,' he said quietly to the guards. 'May God have mercy on his soul.'

The guards nodded, looked through the door at Mo, then wheeled the trolley away. The priest turned away, a tear appearing in one eye. He would go and see the new governor, then he would have to seek out the primate. There were dark days ahead.

Mo was lost in an arid dream when Bobby shook him awake. His head wasn't quite as bad, but the dead camel had given birth to stillborn babies and they too were rotting in his throat. He blinked blearily up into Bobby's bearded face.

'Your bravery will not be forgotten,' Bobby said.

Mo nodded.

It came back to him that he still didn't know the contents of last night's message. Did Mary really love him?

'All the boys are behind you,' Bobby said.

'What about Mary?' Mo whispered.

'She'll be thrilled. So will Tar. This will mend a few bridges, I tell ye.'

Mo's brow furrowed. 'Tar wants to kill me.'

Bobby grabbed his shoulder. 'Not after this, Mo. Not after this! When the message came through last night, nobody was willing to volunteer. We've had hunger strikes before, Mo, but they've never worked out. Volunteers change their minds when the going gets tough. They get sick early on, sometimes make themselves sick so they can come off. We all love Ireland, Mo, we all love the campaign and sticking it to the Brits, but a hunger strike is something else. It's one man, killing himself for what he believes in. It's the ultimate sacrifice. Any fool can get himself shot or blow himself up with a bomb, but taking a decision like this, knowing that you're going to starve yourself to death over the course of what, forty, fifty, sixty days . . . that is true devotion, true bravery, there's only one in a million can handle it. You'll be a saint yet, Mo, you'll be Saint Mo!' He shook Mo's shoulder again. 'I love you like a brother, Mo, I love you like a son. We all do, and we'll see you through this. We'll crack the Brits this time, son, we'll crack them. They won't let a wee lad like you starve himself to death, the whole world will hate them . . . I tell ye, they'll be packin' their bags in the army bases before the month is out. And all because of Saint Mo! Good on ye, son.'

The sound of the trolley banging against a cell door echoed down the corridor. Bobby glanced round, suddenly panicked. 'Sorry, mate,' he said, jumping to his feet, 'I gotta get me breakfast, I'm fuckin' starvin' after last night.'

He hurried to the door, then stopped, looked back and raised a thumb to Mo. 'For Ireland!' he shouted and disappeared after the trolley.

Mo sat up and rubbed his stomach. 'Oh shit,' he said.

15

Every day they came and asked him if he wanted food, but they never brought it. They knew his pedigree and his history. They presumed in advance that he would say no, that they merely had to be seen to be trying to persuade him to come off his hunger strike. If they had arrived with toast or ham or Sugar Frosties or Opal Fruits he would have gobbled them down, but all they brought were polite requests and politically wrapped pleadings, and neither of them tickled his tastebuds.

When he was tempted to say, Yes, give me some sausages, he felt the eyes of his comrades upon him, even through the walls, and couldn't go through with it. He was resigned to Ireland killing him.

By the fourth day he no longer felt hungry; he drank water, sometimes salted, sometimes not. He had a mild headache. There was a new governor. He was known as Rat II, although to Mo's ear it sounded like ratatouille, which only made him hungrier. He was tall and gaunt and as nervous as a man whose three predecessors had all been murdered should be.

'How are you feeling?' he asked Mo, sitting on the edge of his bed.

'Hungry,' said Mo, without a smile.

Rat II nodded and said, 'Is there anything I can get you?'

'Food,' said Mo, and Rat II nodded but made no move. It was lunchtime and the smells of roast beef and carrots and thick sticky toffee pudding wafted along the corridor and besieged the closed door of his cell.

'You know,' Rat II said, 'there is room to manoeuvre on several of your demands.'

'I haven't made any demands,' said Mo.

Rat II nodded. 'But Tar McAdam has,' he said.

'Of course,' said Mo.

His attention was drawn to the floor. There was a beetle scuttling across. If the governor hadn't been with him he would have had it in his mouth. Sucking it. Making it last. Or holding it captive in his locker. Eating a leg at a time. His mouth was watering, his eyes bulging . . . he forced himself to look at the governor's face. No meat there. His cheeks were drawn in, like he was trying to suck the life out of a gobstopper. *A gobstopper.* A meal within a meal within a meal within a meal, layer after layer after layer after layer . . . like an eyeball. He looked at Rat II's eyeballs. Blue eyes. He would suck the colour out of them first. Their flavour would be *blue*, and the rest would be juicy, meaty, with jelly. Jelly, jelly and ice cream. With wafers. What did they have at the seaside? A thick wodge of ice cream between two wafers – a *slider*. Or a cone with a Flake rammed in the top. A *ninety-nine*.

The ancient woman in the ice cream van with the big set of jangly keys and cobwebs in her hair, handing over the poke, the lemon top, the bitter taste, the beautiful bitter taste . . .

'We can't get the troops out, you know that.'

'I know that.'

'But we can get them to be a bit more pleasant. Good manners cost nothing.'

Mo nodded.

'And this nonsense about renouncing our claims to Northern Ireland. We can't do that. We have a responsibility to one million Protestants, and quite a few atheists. Look what happened in the Falklands, for God's sake. We just can't do it. But we'll agree to call Londonderry Derry, if it makes you happy. There, that's a concession. You've been asking for that for years. Can't argue with that, can you?'

Mo shook his head. 'All I want is a uniform that fits.'

'Yes, I heard that story. On the surface such a simple request, but the ramifications, dear boy, the ramifications. God, we'd have tailors in here day in, day out. Is that lapel wide enough for you, sir?

A little less flared, perhaps? What about the drain-pipe look, it's all the rage.' Rat II laughed, nervously. 'Sorry,' he said, 'but you take my point.'

Mo nodded wearily.

'Your grandfather seems a sensible chap,' Rat II said.

'You've spoken to him?'

'I've pleaded with him. You understand that when you do eventually lapse into a coma he has the right to bring you off your hunger strike. We'll have needles in your arms and half a crate of Lucozade down you before you can shout chucky or whatever it is you shout. You know that?'

Mo nodded.

'Although he says he won't interfere with your right to die a horrible death.'

Mo shrugged.

'You do know what happens, right near the end? You lose control of the muscles in your head.'

'Head muscles?' Mo asked.

'Eye muscles. Your eyes just flop out of your face. Sit on your cheek. I've seen it happen. They just sit there. Quivering.'

'And can you still see through them?'

'I don't know. Never asked. Suppose you can. You'll be able to tell me. For God's sake, son, take a bit of toast. I'll sneak it in. No one need ever know. The longer we can prolong this, the better chance there is of a settlement, although right now there's no chance of a settlement. Will you have some?'

Mo shook his head. 'I can't.'

'Can.'

'Can't.'

'Can.'

'Can't.'

'Please, son, I've got Tin Knickers breathing down my neck.'

'You call her that as well?'

'Everyone calls her that. Even her husband, I'll bet. She's keeping a close eye on you. She phones every day. At least someone in her office does. But I know she's concerned. You're getting a lot of press. Good and bad. But mostly bad. There's very little sympathy out there. And damn all in here. You're not winning any friends. And don't make the mistake of thinking all of these boys in here with you are your friends. You choose your friends in this life, you don't have them thrust upon you. I wouldn't trust one of them as far as I could throw him. What kind of friends let a little boy starve himself to death instead of them? Tell me that.'

'I don't know,' said Mo.

'If you think you'll win their respect by doing this, well maybe you will, but it'll be damn all use to you when you're six feet under. We can put it on your gravestone. *Respected by many, mourned by few*. We won't be letting them out for your funeral, put it that way. Am I boring you?'

'No.'

'That's good. Anyway,' he looked at his watch, 'work to do. Will you think about what I said?'

Mo nodded, though he had no idea what Rat II had said. All he knew was that he had survived for much longer than this in the desert; there'd been no water at all and the heat had been murderous. At least the Kesh was cool and he had salt water to drink. He would survive indefinitely, if he didn't die first.

16

Several hundred miles away, in a house that looked deceptively small from the outside, a cantankerous old busybody called Sir Thomas Earpole was pushing his weary legs up the stairs to meet another cantankerous old busybody known universally as Tin Knickers. He was her personal private secretary, she was his hero. Or heroine. He loved her like he loved no other woman, and he loved no other woman. Not even his wife, who was small and blonde and getting smaller all the time since her death. He was eighty if he was a day, and he was definitely a day, usually a Monday; a blue Monday, small and dark and depressingly full of no-hope for the coming week. She had detailed him personally to phone the prison every day to ask after the health of the child Mohammed Maguire. She abhorred all terrorism, and all terrorists, but she had a soft spot for Mohammed Maguire. His mother had been one of the most feared terrorists of her generation, and one of the best double agents MI6 had ever had. The information she had been able to provide had helped decimate not only the ranks of the IRA but also those of a number of other international terrorist organisations, culminating in an assault on a training camp in Libya that had led to her own death. She had betrayed her comrades, not only because she was disillusioned with their violence but also because she was disillusioned with herself and her lack of nationalistic fervour. It had been a teenage thing, like Christianity or the Bay City Rollers; she had grown out of it, but had been stuck with the old records, the old flares, the old baggage. Except there had been an alternative; she had sought it out and had no qualms about turning sides. She wanted her child, a son of terrorism, to grow up without it, but for her to work effectively as a double agent she had to continue to work effectively as a terrorist, so she bombed and killed and maimed in the name of peace, much as Tar McAdam continued to do, except she had meant it.

The prime minister smiled at the doddery old man coming towards her. She poured two glasses of Scotch, handed him one, then flicked at some fluff on her blue suit while he looked admiringly at her legs through the bottom of his glass.

'How is the boy?' she asked between sips. She patted the top of a sofa, indicating that he should sit. She sat opposite him. He continued to look at her legs.

'Going downhill,' said Sir Thomas.

She nodded. 'We cannot allow him to die. We owe him his life, even if he doesn't know it. What of the Mountain Climber?'

Sir Thomas shook his head. 'Getting nowhere.'

'He conveyed our offer?'

'Conveyed, rejected. He says the boy's very

smart, holding to his own line. The other criminals have little influence over him. Rather the other way around.'

'He's his mother's boy.'

'Did you ever meet her, Prime Minister?'

'Once. At an army base in Scotland. She had the boy with her. Of course he was very small. We had tea. A remarkable woman.'

'As you are yourself.'

'Why, thank you, Sir Thomas. But what shall we do?'

Sir Thomas shook his head. 'Prime Minister, the doctors don't give him long. He's not strong. If he dies, it will be bad for us. The press here are on our side, of course, but internationally . . . well, you know how it is with the Americans.'

'Damn the Americans.' Her voice was suddenly hard. Almost ragged. He had noticed it getting that way again in recent months. Pre-election they had persuaded her to soften it, tone it down for television, but now the old harshness was creeping back. He quite liked it like that.

'Indeed, damn the lot of them.'

'Whether they like it or not, and whether he likes it or not, he's a British subject and we're responsible for him. When she wasn't killing people his mother was a loyal and trusted servant of the Crown. We must help in any way we can.' She shook her head sadly. 'The question remains, what are we to do?'

'The nationalists are mobilising behind him. There'll be civil war if he dies.'

'There's practically civil war now, Sir Thomas; that doesn't concern me. It's how to get the boy out that concerns me.'

'There is a campaign to free him. It hasn't gained much support yet, but it claims to have evidence that his confession was fabricated.'

'And was it?'

'They usually are.'

'Well, shall we go down that route?'

'We don't normally consider that route for at least eighteen years. Anything less than that will seem like weakness.'

'And we can't be seen to be weak.'

'No, Prime Minister.'

'Hmmm.' She pursed her lips. She took another sip. Her tongue darted out and in again. Sir Thomas watched it through the bottom of his glass. 'I must think some more about this. Can I get you another, Sir Thomas?'

Sir Thomas nodded and passed his glass across to the prime minister. As she poured he said, 'Of course we could release, through informal channels, the information about his mother being our agent.'

'They'd dismiss it as disinformation.'

'I'm sure there are photographs, tapes. There usually are. They wouldn't feel so strongly about him then.'

'But it would destroy him.'

'It might save him.'

'But save him for what?'

'I don't know, Prime Minister.'

She shook her head. 'No. I gave her my word that he would never know. And I always keep my word.'

'Indeed you do, irrespective of whether the circumstances that caused you to give your word in the first place have changed.'

The prime minister smiled tightly. 'Why, you old cynic, Sir Thomas.'

'Ma'am,' he said, giving a mock bow.

'I will need to think about this, Sir Thomas.'

The old man nodded. 'Don't take too long. He may not have very much longer left.'

He stood, with some difficulty, and handed his glass to the prime minister. She looked at it for a moment then drained the mouthful he had left at the bottom. As he reached the doorway he stopped, then turned slowly back towards her. He paused for a moment, and she raised an eyebrow.

'Sir Thomas?'

'Be careful, Prime Minister, we could lose Northern Ireland over this.'

She nodded thoughtfully. 'Yes, Sir Thomas, I realise that. But then there's a plus side to every crisis.'

17

His eyes flickered. The light was no longer neon but it still hurt. It was a bedside lamp, like he was at home and could sit up and read a book on his day off sick from school. Except he'd never really had a home or a lamp and he couldn't read a book because he hadn't gone to school much and this sickness was of his own making. It was the thirtieth day. His weight had dropped *way down*. Doctors kept a constant watch on him. Rat II came every hour. Bobby, elected as the prisoners' representative, sat by his bed. His grandfather was outside, in a waiting room, picking losers from the racing section of the *Irish News*.

The priest had given him the last rites on several occasions in the past week, which, he appreciated, was something of a contradiction in terms, although the second-next-to-last rites didn't have the same ring to it. The priest was doing his best for a young man who didn't believe in God.

'Do you think it just ends, and there's nothing else?' he asked Mo in one of his – Mo's – occasional moments of lucidity. Mo rolled his eyes – although not too much, in case they fell out of their sockets and sat on his bony cheeks like buoys in a pale, calm bay – and said, 'Oh just cheer me up.' Bobby giggled in the corner.

The priest shrugged. 'The Lord God loves us all,' he said.

'He doesn't love me,' said Mo. 'I been evil since day one.'

'You're not evil, Mo.'

'Yes I am. It's in my genes.'

'Don't be daft.'

'I'm going straight to hell.'

The priest thought for a moment. 'How can you go to hell if you don't believe in God?'

'Because I believe in evil and not in goodness.'

'That's wild philosophical for a wee lad like yourself.'

'I've had time to think.'

'It's so depressing.'

'You should try swapping places.'

'If I could I would.'

'Would you really?'

The priest blinked nervously. He swallowed, then crossed his fingers beyond Mo's eyeline. 'If I thought it would achieve something.'

Mo shook his head slowly. 'It's a little late for that.'

The priest, relieved, shook his head regretfully. 'You're throwing your life away, Mo, for nothing.'

'He's not throwing it away for nothing,' Bobby said from his chair, 'he's throwing it away for Ireland.'

'And do you really think the Brits will take the slightest bit of notice, Bobby?'

'Have you looked outside lately, Father? There's five thousand people out there holding five thousand candles, all for Mohammed Maguire.'

'Candles go out,' the priest responded. 'Then there'll just be a lot of depressed people with wax on their hands.'

'For a man of God you've very little faith, Father.'

'On the contrary, I've a lot of faith – in God. Not so much in people.'

'You think we want Mo to die, don't you?'

'I don't think you want him to die as a person, you want him to die as a symbol. Unfortunately the two are inextricably linked.'

'If I could swap places with him, believe me I would,' Bobby said.

'Feel free,' said Mo.

'Unfortunately,' Bobby said, ignoring him, 'Mo chose to take this on himself. To make the ultimate sacrifice. There is no greater thing a man can do for Ireland than to starve himself to death.' A bell sounded distantly, out by the cells, away from this hospital wing, and Bobby jumped up. 'Now, if you'll excuse me, that's lunch. I'll be back shortly.'

Bobby half bowed at Mo, nodded at the priest and knocked on the door for an escort back to the wings. When he had gone the priest said, 'Is there anything I can do to make you more comfortable, Mo?'

Mo shook his head. The hunger had long gone now. All he wanted to do was sleep. When he woke he would be with his mother and father. There would be no war. No bombs. No guns. Not in heaven, not even in hell. Just somewhere in between where they could enjoy a normal life, like Belgium. In front of the fire. Reading a book. Drinking Ribena and eating ham sandwiches. With a promise of chocolate to come.

A doctor came in to check his vital signs.

'How are they?' the priest asked.

'Vital,' said the doctor, and left.

Rat II put his head around the door. 'Chin up,' he said mysteriously, then departed.

Mo closed his eyes. He had no idea how long had passed when he opened them again. The priest was still there, standing at the foot of his bed, hands clasped, praying quietly. To his left his grandfather sat, hands folded in his lap, staring at the floor. To his right . . . *Mary*?

She smiled at him. 'Hiya,' she said.

'Mary,' he said weakly. 'How's the campaign going?'

'Great. If you released a single now, it would go straight to number one.'

'Can't sing. Can't dance. Ask Bobby.'

'When we get you out of here, I'll teach you to dance.'

'Is that a promise?'

'That's a promise.'

'I might be a little stiff. And you'll have to get the nails out of the box.'

'Don't say that, Mo.'

'You see the British caving in?'

'They have to. They won't let you die. They just like to leave things to the last possible moment.'

'Don't lie to me, Mary.'

'I'm not. Not really.'

He smiled. His teeth felt loose.

'I'm so proud of you,' she said.

'I'm proud of you too. You kissed me once.'

'I know.'

'Would you kiss me again?'

'I would.'

She came along the side of the bed towards him. She bent down to him. Her dark red hair fell over his face. Her lips caressed his dry and brittle lips. Her tongue darted onto his desert tongue, the moisture of it creating a fleeting oasis. When she pulled away he said, 'That girl's wearing Harmony Hair Spray,' and she smiled and blushed.

He closed his eyes.

18

The Chinook took off from Fort George, near Inverness, just after 7 p.m. It was dark and it was raining heavily, as it always seemed to in that part of the world. Tin Knickers was attending a security conference, or was supposed to be. She stayed for the opening remarks, the first speech, and then when the slide show had begun she slipped out with her bodyguards and raced to the waiting helicopter.

It took just twenty-five minutes to cross the

narrow strip of choppy sea to Northern Ireland. The skies were clearer on the other side and she was able to reclaim her stomach before the helicopter touched down in the grounds of the Maze. As they descended she thought for a moment that her eyes were playing tricks; she could see the ground getting closer, could pick out the details, but the lights of the city seemed to remain constant in size, tiny and . . .

'Candles, Prime Minister,' a bodyguard said.

'Candles?'

'A vigil for the boy. They're candles.'

'Oh. I see.' She nodded. There was a suggestion of a tear in her eye. Just a suggestion. For it to progress actually to being a tear it would have had to prostrate itself before the several dour and disciplined selection committees that sat constantly in her conscience. This time the application was rejected, but it was noted and recommended to try again at a later date.

The Chinook touched down on one of the all-weather football pitches. To protect her from prying eyes she wore a black trenchcoat and an umbrella was pulled down tight around her, though it was no longer raining. She was hurried across the astro-turf into the administration centre and then straight to Rat II's office. He had laid on tea and biscuits and prepared his comments well. She nodded appreciatively as he spoke, but she was barely listening. Hours, not days, Sir Thomas Earpole had told her, and she had made the decision to come against all advice. It wasn't her coming to the prison that they objected to, it was the coming and failing to persuade him off the protest. That would be too much. They muttered angrily that Tin Knickers was wetting them over a scrawny Irish rebel.

'His family is with him?'

'His grandfather. A girl who claims to be his cousin but is in fact a courier for Tar McAdam. Then there's the other criminals, lining up to be the next to join the hunger strike if Mo dies. That's it. Plus the ten thousand outside.'

'I thought it was five.'

'It was.'

The prime minister nodded. 'Then take me to him.'

Rat II nodded. He finished a custard cream then lifted the phone and called the hospital wing.

'You can't fucking do this!' Bobby shouted. But they hit him with a baton, and then they did. They removed him back to his cell. They were politer with the grandfather and the girl, moving them to the waiting room where they could watch live coverage of the vigil on the television in the corner. They were locked in.

The corridors were cleared of all but the Rat's most trusted prison officers, which left two in charge of the hospital wing. Even the doctors were excluded, and they went back to running their book on how long Mo would survive.

Rat II and the guards paused at the door to Mo's room. Tin Knickers stood, looking at the bed, at the tiny, emaciated figure lying in it, the covers thrown back. She shook her head slowly. 'What a waste,' she whispered.

Rat II nodded beside her.

'Do you have a key to this room?' the prime minister asked.

'Why, yes,' said Rat II.

'Give me it.' She put out her hand. Rat II looked to one of his guards and nodded. He handed it to her. 'Thank you,' she said. 'Now, if you don't mind, I would like to be alone with him.'

'But Prime—'

And the look she gave him was steely enough for him to stop and step back from the door. She nodded once then entered the room. She closed the door and locked it. There were no windows, no daylight, no surveillance cameras. She stood at the end of the bed for several long moments, looking at him. His breathing was soft and easy, but every once in a while he coughed and pain etched itself on his face.

'Mohammed Maguire,' she called softly. There was no response. 'Mohammed Maguire,' she called again, harder this time. Nothing. 'Mohammed Maguire!' she barked.

His eyes shot open. It took him several moments to focus. Longer to recognise. 'I *have* gone to hell,' he whispered.

She moved along the side of the bed, pulled a

chair up and grasped his hand. It was like shaking hands with a sparrow. She swallowed hard. 'Mohammed Maguire,' she said, 'you must stop this.'

'It's too late,' he whispered.

'No it's not, not at all.'

'My uniform, it doesn't fit.'

'You don't need one, Mohammed. Not where you're going.'

'No uniforms in hell.'

'Not hell, Hollywood. Perhaps it's the same.'

'I told the Mountain Climber . . .'

'Now tell me.'

'I can't . . .'

'You can. It's what your mother would have wanted . . .'

He gave a weak, dry, raspy laugh. 'She would have wanted me to die.'

She squeezed his hand. 'No, she wouldn't, Mohammed. She would have wanted you to live.'

'Die for Ireland.'

'Live for peace.'

He shook his head. 'You don't know my . . .'

'But I did. Mohammed, she worked for us. For the British government.'

'Your old arse is a tit, she did.'

'I swear to God, Mo. She was a double agent. She hated all of this. She was working for peace.'

Mo laughed. 'I'm not a fool.'

'No. No, you're not. You're young and brave and full of anger and hatred, but I'm not lying to you. She worked for us.'

'Ballbags.'

'I can prove it to you. I can provide video evidence. She gave us hours and hours of sworn testimony on video. It's why Tar McAdam had her killed.'

'Tar—'

'Yes, Mohammed. She was supposed to leave that camp in Libya before the Marines attacked; she had tipped us off about it. But Tar McAdam ordered her to stay. And because she stayed your father stayed, and because they both stayed they both died. Your war isn't with the British or the Americans, it's with your own leader.'

'He's not my leader.'

'That's the spirit.'

'He was *never* my leader.'

'Then come off the hunger strike.'

'I can't, the boys are depending . . .'

'They're depending on nothing! They're criminals, Mohammed, killers and robbers and . . .
They're not dying for Ireland, are they, Mo, why
should you?'

'Because . . .'

'Because they forced you into it. You may think
you volunteered, but did you really have any
choice? You were manoeuvred into it, Mohammed,
now you must allow me to manoeuvre you out
of it. Your mother gave her life for peace, Mo,
peace. I'm not asking you to do that, I'm just asking
you to eat, so that you can weigh up the evidence
yourself. Don't die for the wrong reason, Mo.'

'Because I'd regret it for the rest of my life.'

She smiled. 'Give yourself a chance.'

'Are you serious about my mum?'

She nodded.

'Really, really serious? Cross your heart and hope
to die?'

'Cross my heart and hope to die. She could tell no one. It was too dangerous. She was the bravest woman I ever met. And I think you are the bravest boy.'

He looked at her and a tear appeared in his eye. It rolled down his cheek. 'I just want her back,' he said softly. He closed his eyes to stop the tears coming back, but it was no use.

She stood. Her tear ducts had gained permission. They ran down her cheeks and splashed onto her blue suit. She took the suit jacket off. And then her skirt. She was standing in her underwear. She turned to the door. She tried the handle, making sure it was locked.

Outside Rat II saw the handle move and jumped to attention. When the door didn't open he said, 'Everything okay in there?'

'Fine,' came her clipped reply.

The prime minister crossed back to the bed. She pulled the quilt further back then slipped into the bed beside Mohammed Maguire. She put her arm around his frail shoulder and lifted him onto her chest. He gave a little moan of pain then settled down, his head against her breast. She began to stroke his damp hair. She pulled the quilt over them and began to hum softly, something tuneless but soothing. Very soon he was asleep.

Thirty minutes later, fully dressed, she left the room. The doctors, fearing the worst, that they had missed the moment of death and had forfeited their bets, stood nervously beside Rat II.

'Okay,' the prime minister said, 'you can begin to feed him again.'

Rat II's mouth dropped open. 'He's agreed . . .'

'He's agreed. Now get me out of here, I've a country to run.'

She turned and began to walk off down the corridor.

'But Prime Minister,' one of the doctors called after her, 'he has to sign this to give his permission.'

She stopped, she turned. 'I've told you to start feeding him. Now start. He'll sign later.'

'Yes, Prime Minister,' said the doctor.

The Ledge

'God,' said Santa, 'I didn't know the half of that.'

It was getting late. Sandwiches had been passed out to them. The camera crews had moved on to different, less static stories. They'd pooled their resources and left behind a clot with a video camera to record the jump if it ever happened, but they doubted that it ever would. Not after all this time.

It was Christmas, for God's sake. There was a frost settling on the ground and on the ledge and on Inspector Campbell's bald pate. There were fairy lights across the way. The whole world glistened and glowed.

'You'll be used to this,' Inspector Campbell said to Santa, nodding at the enchanting surroundings.

'Don't be so fucking stupid,' Santa snapped back, and they all looked at him. Santa turned away, bending to the plate of sandwiches that sat precariously on the window ledge, although not as precariously as the unlikely squad devouring them. Mo picked one up as well. He swallowed it in one.

'You've got your appetite back then,' said Mr Clarke.

'What?'

'After the hunger strike.'

'Of course I bloody got it back. It was ten years ago.'

'That long? Gosh. How time flies.'

'You've put weight on,' observed Inspector Campbell.

'Of course I've put weight on!'

'You went to America, right?' said Santa. 'I remember that much.'

'Did you make a movie?' asked Inspector Campbell. 'I remember hearing that you were going to make a movie.'

'No,' said Mo, 'I didn't make a movie. Things didn't work out.'

'Is that why you're out here?' asked Santa.

'No, that's not why I'm out here.'

'Is it about the bear?' asked Mr Clarke.

19

So one day Spielberg was on the phone.

How long after? Three months, maybe. He'd put most of the weight back on. He even had a bit of a tan. Thank God for Michael Calhoon, not that there was a God. The prime minister had been as good as her word. *Tin Knickers.* He called her that. Not to her face, because he never saw her face again. But over the phone. Long distance to LA. She called him, once a month. Or sometimes he called her. *Hello, could I speak to Tin Knickers?* And they knew, he didn't even have to say his name, because nobody else dared call her Tin Knickers. And she called him Mo. She loved him like the son she never had.

Even Sir Thomas Earpole noticed the difference in her. When Mo phoned her voice softened. Her cheeks coloured. Her eyes glinted. She asked about his weight and his reading – he was reading *everything* now that Calhoon had employed a personal tutor – and even gave him a reading list. Her regard for him didn't make up for the fact that everyone in Ireland wanted to kill him, but it lessened the pain. All over the little island earnest patriots were cursing his name and starving themselves to death to prove that they weren't all as fickle as Mohammed Maguire. There was one hundred thousand dollars on his head, and more if you could provide the rest, still breathing, so that Tar McAdam could kill him personally.

He had had enough of Ireland. His mother had betrayed Ireland, and now so had he. This was a new start, a new beginning. This was America.

*　　*　　*

Mohammed Maguire

There was a swimming pool. And he could dive in first thing in the morning and not have to worry about whether someone had left a shite in the bottom like at home. And that made him think of Sandy and how much he would have loved America. The heat and the friendliness. They could have sniffed unleaded gasoline; it would have been both cheaper and healthier.

Calhoon had a wife now, a blonde Texan with breasts the size of crusty loaves and a job selling ceramic tiles. She couldn't understand a word Mo said, though he did his best to temper his accent, but she was nice and friendly and didn't tell Calhoon when she caught him smoking dope in the garage. Calhoon wasn't there much anyway. He was off all day selling Ireland to the studios. There were tax breaks to be had for filming in Ireland, and the Irish didn't mind how ridiculous they were made to look. *The Quiet Man*? No problem. *Ryan's Daughter*. Come on in. And then one day he was talking to Spielberg and happened to mention Mo, and a little light came on and a meeting was set up by the end of the day.

ET. Raiders. Jaws.

None of those.

Sid Spielberg, a distant second cousin, a lapsed Hasidic Jew, with the beard, without the faith, on the razzle in Hollywood and with nothing but the name in common with his illustrious relative, not even good relations. But the initial S and the surname Spielberg helped him up those first few rungs of the ladder where chutzpah was more important than money or talent. Thereafter he'd stalled: there were some TV movies, some soft porn, a few straight-to-video martial arts, even a no-budget thriller that won an award at a small festival in Albuquerque.

He raced up to Calhoon's house in a Porsche with three poodles in the back. He charmed Mo with his charm. He took him to a baseball game. Mo discovered that baseball bats had other uses besides breaking legs. He bought him hotdogs and comics, he encouraged Mo to see movies – though he studiously avoided showing him his own – and to think about becoming an actor. Not for the first time the idea of Mo starring in his own story was floated. A screen test was set up and the idea of Mo starring in his own story was not raised again.

Mo didn't care. Now that he could read, he discovered writing. With a vengeance. He was in Hollywood. He wanted to write for the movies. He had *loved* the movies with his mother, the thrill of seeing something splendid on the big screen, or the excitement of bombing the cinema if it was crap. Sid gave him a book on writing screenplays. In eight days Mo penned *Donaghadee Ninja*, the true story, he claimed, of Wee Sammy Nutt, born and reared in the dull Northern Irish coastal town of Donaghadee, who, by a twist of fate, became one of the Orient's most feared ninjas. Although Wee Sammy carried the characteristic double-edged sword of the ninja, he forsook their hooded, mysterious appearance for one even more likely to strike the fear of God into his victims: Doc Martens, parallels and a tight curly perm. Although this was considered pretty chic in Donaghadee, he did stand out a bit in Peking's Forbidden Palace. His catch phrase was 'Variety is the rice of life'.

Sid took one look at the screenplay and advised Mo to stick to acting.

His advice fell on deaf ears. Mo, by now sniffing around cocaine addiction, which he financed by selling pints of his blood to a clinic off Sunset Boulevard, produced a screenplay a week for six weeks. He came up with a variation on *Lassie* featuring a red setter instead of a collie. Red setters, he argued, are the only dogs that are genuinely bonkers. They spend their whole lives charging across busy roads in pursuit of animals that have never existed.

Sid, his eyes fixed squarely on getting the rights to *The Mohammed Maguire Story* in the bag, even set up a meeting for Mo to pitch one of his screenplays to a producer at Fox.

Jimmy Fox, that was, like Sid on the outside wanting in. He liked to show off what Hollywood had done for him, but it had done nothing. He'd won everything in the lottery. Jimmy, gone-to-seed flash, was intrigued by the notion of a fifteen-year-old screenwriter and gave him his chance. 'Okay, kid, shoot,' he said, lolling by his pool, though it really wasn't the best thing to say round Mohammed Maguire.

Mo, tanned, high, eyes rolling, launched into it. 'Well, y'see – y'see, it's about my uncle, my late uncle. He was an explorer. Polar. Polar exploration.'

'Expensive,' Jimmy Fox said, already thinking of the location budget, though he'd never had a location budget in his life.

'He led the first expedition to the North Pole by donkey.'

'Donkey?'

'Donkey.'

'This is comedy, right?'

'No. Tragedy.'

Jimmy Fox lit another cigar.

'He knew he'd need a special breed of man,' Mo said, 'not to mention the donkeys. Men who would be hardy, strong, brave, yet intelligent, gentle and caring; men who believed in what they were doing, who cared about their donkeys and could knit fresh socks for themselves. Men who could shake their fists at fate and shout, "Amputate my arms," when they meant their legs. To this end he placed an advert in the local paper. "Wanted: Strong hairy men with interest in donkeys for hazardous journey. Not much chance of survival. Ring Belfast 3861 after 7 p.m."'

Jimmy nodded. Mo was walking along the side of the pool, playing it all out. Jimmy, under cover of his stomach, punched numbers into his mobile phone. Sid Spielberg answered.

'Sid? Jimmy. Sid, what sort of a freakin' idiot have you sent me?'

'Listen, Jimmy, a favour, all right already?'

'I'll do him a favour, I'll have him locked up. You get over here, you get the . . . shit, here he comes . . .'

'The team was recruited remarkably quickly and set off without the glare of publicity. Their first stop was Belfast Central railway station where a fellow passenger recorded my uncle's legendary farewell speech to an astonished conductor: "Three returns to the North Pole please, and two halfs for the donkeys."' Mo paused. 'Are you following this?'

'I'm following this,' said Jimmy.

'And what do you think so far?'

'I'm intrigued.'

'My accent isn't too strong, is it? I can slow down.'

'No. Not at all. Speed up, if you want.'

Mo smiled. He was getting there. 'They made good time, but progress was slow. My uncle was full of meaningless observations like that. There were others: *It is snowing, but we have no tin-opener. We're all suffering from frost bite, but at least the donkeys have their hay. Time seems to stand still up here, which is just as well as we have no watches.* You're still with me?'

'I'm hangin' in there.'

'Good, this is the climax now. A mystery at the end, 'cause no one really knows what happened to them. His diary, discovered only yards from base camp, soaked in blood, contained one last despairing entry that gave some little clue to his fate: *Even as I struggle to scrawl these last few words, the donkeys are gnawing at my legs. It is better to have lived and died than not to have lived at all, unless you're a Presbyterian.*'

Mo looked eagerly for some sort of reaction. 'It's still fairly rough,' he said.

'Mmmm,' said Jimmy, 'have a banana.'

There was a large fruit basket sitting by his sun lounger, and there was a smaller one talking about the North Pole and donkeys.

Mo took a banana and sat on the edge of the pool, dangling his feet in the warm water.

Jimmy looked at him for several moments, then said, 'Why don't you take your shoes off?'

If he heard, Mo didn't respond. Instead he toppled forward and sank slowly to the bottom.

Jimmy jumped out of his seat and peered into the pool. 'Hey, kid,' he called, 'quit freakin' around.'

There was no response. Save for a few bubbles breaking the surface.

'Freakin' hell,' said Jimmy.

20

Later he would come to equate the turning points in his life with waking up. In the desert, waking up to the Bedouin. In the prison, waking up to the hunger strike. In America, waking up in the hospital with a grim-faced man in a white coat nodding at him. Cocooned in sleep; nobody could touch him. Safety. Sleep. With Mum and Dad. Mom and Pop. Sacrilege. *Sacrilege?* No. *Sanctuary.* He rolled over, away from him, but something snagged at his arm and there was a twinge of pain.

He rolled back. There was a drip tube leading from his arm.

'Would you like a drink of H_2O,' the man in the white coat said.

His throat, as per usual, was desert dry. 'I'd like a drink of water,' Mo rasped.

'H_2O is water,' the man said.

'I know,' said Mo.

The man in the white coat got up and poured him a glass from a plastic bottle that sat on a locker by his bed. Mo glugged it greedily. 'What happened?' Mo asked as he handed the empty glass back.

'You fell in a swimming pool, nearly drowned.'

'Oh,' said Mo.

'My name is Oswald Tarantino. I'm a psychiatrist. I've been reading your file.'

'I have a file?'

'*Everybody* has a file.'

'So what does it say?'

'Too much. Way too much. You've had a busy life, and you're only fifteen.'

'Fourteen and a half,' said Mo.

Tarantino smiled. 'We'll soon have you feeling happy as Larry.'

'Who's Larry?' asked Mo.

'Larry Fortemeyer in the next bed.' Mo looked to the next bed. It was empty. 'Larry's nuts,' said Tarantino. 'He thinks he's invisible.'

Mo nodded.

'He's just gone for a shower,' Tarantino added.

Mo held out his glass. Tarantino poured. 'Has anyone been to see me?'

Tarantino shrugged. 'Couldn't say. Lots of people came to see Larry, I know that much.'

'And did they?'

'And did they what?'

'See him.'

'I have no idea. I think we're getting off the track here, Mohammed.'

'You can call me Mo.'

'I know I can. You obviously have a problem with Mohammed.'

Mo shook his head. 'It's shorter.'

'You have a problem with length?'

'Not that I'm aware of.'

'What about a length of the pool?'

'What pool?'

'The pool you tried to commit suicide in.'

'I tried to commit suicide?'

'It says it right here, in your file.'

'Well, who wrote the file?'

Tarantino studied the file. 'Mmmm,' he said. 'Good point. It appears that I did.' He nodded at his own handwriting for several long moments. 'Okay,' he said eventually, 'I remember now. The man who brought you in said you tried to kill yourself.'

'And who's he when he's at home?'

'When he's at home I don't know, when he was downstairs he said his name was Fox. He was soaking wet. He was very upset. He said you tried to kill yourself because he wasn't interested in your screenplays.'

Mo shrugged. 'It's no reason to kill yourself.'

Tarantino nodded in agreement. 'If everyone who wrote screenplays in this town tried to kill themselves there'd be bodies everywhere. People wouldn't be able to drown themselves for dead bodies clogging up the pool. This is LA. Everyone writes screenplays. My son, he's twelve, he writes screenplays. You're not so young. What were your screenplays about? You don't have to tell me.'

'Polar exploration.'

'Happy ending?'

Mo shook his head. Tarantino made a note. 'Another one was about a red setter.'

'A dog?'

'A dog. Mad dog. Ended up drowning in a reservoir.'

Reservoir, noted Tarantino. *Dogs. Not a happy ending.* 'There's a pattern emerging here. You're not happy, are you, Mohammed?'

Mo shrugged. 'I never thought about it.'

'Perhaps you should. Although I warn you, it could be very depressing. I have your blood results here. Cocaine. Marijuana. I've seen worse. We have to get you into a programme.'

Mo nodded. 'A self-help programme.'

'A television programme. A documentary. Fly on the wall. We're making one about the hospital.

Hollywood 911 we're calling it. Do you mind if we interview you?'

'I'd rather not.'

'It could be therapeutic. National exposure often is. America loves a loser. But only when he becomes a winner. It's amazing, honestly. Once you see your pathetic little problems exposed in the cold light of videotape, and then they cut to a beer commercial, you begin to realise that life's what you make it, not what it makes you. Take my advice, Mohammed, talk to the team. What good can I possibly do you? Some platitudes, some prescriptions, an electric shock if you're lucky. But you've been around, you've survived, you can sort this out yourself. Unburden yourself. Tell them all about it. Tell them everything.'

Tarantino was obviously deranged, but he had a point. Mo needed to tell someone. He had only ever told anyone little bits and pieces. Spared them the detail. Let it all build up. He had very nearly taken it to the grave with him. Now it sat in his head like a breezeblock, weighing him down, although not enough to keep him at the bottom of a swimming pool. Get it out, lance the boil, suck out the snakebite. Start again. America. Be a winner. Reclaim your soul. Tell *everyone*.

'Okay,' he said, 'I'll do it.'

'No you fucking won't!' the producer yelled as soon as he heard. 'Sodomy in the desert? Shit on the walls? Are you fucking nuts? We can't put that out on the network. We'll be hung up by the fucking balls. Sorry, kid, you're just too fucking weird for us.' He turned to his director. 'Okay, Tom, we'll go with Larry instead. Has anyone seen Larry?'

The director shook his head. The sound recordist shook his head. The cameraman shook his head. Mo's whole life seemed to be filled with people shaking their heads. He went back to bed.

21

'That's one hell of a long shower,' Mo was saying, nodding at the next bed.

'Cleanliness is next to godliness,' said Tarantino, 'and you're getting off the track again. You have to face these things, Mohammed, or they'll crush you.'

'They *have* crushed me. That's why I'm here.'

Tarantino tutted and made a note. He sucked on the end of his pen. 'What do you remember about the desert, Mohammed?'

'Did Tar McAdam send you?'

'What?'

'Nothing. Doesn't matter.' Mo sighed. He shrugged. 'This and that. Walking from dusk till dawn.'

From dusk till dawn, wrote Tarantino. Mo told him about sodomy, the Bedouin and their death.

'And when you killed them, do you think that was something you were able to do only because of what they did to you, or was it something that was always inside you?'

'You mean my pedigree. My parents.' Mo shrugged again. Then laughed. 'I suppose I'm just a natural born killer.'

Tarantino made a note.

'Have you come to any conclusions, Doc?' Mo asked after the interview had rambled on for a further thirty minutes.

Tarantino took another suck at his pen. 'I don't want to scare you, but I'm pretty much convinced that you *are* a psycho.'

'And what do you do with psychos?' Mo asked. 'Lock them up?'

Tarantino nodded. 'Or get them an agent. It depends how the psychosis manifests itself. Some of our greatest talents have been psychos. No one's going to tell me Marlon Brando's Mr Normal. Or Robin Williams. Now there's a man could benefit from some shock therapy. It's all around us, Mohammed. Jack Nicholson? Orson Welles? Meryl Streep?'

'Meryl Streep?'

'Fucking right. Schizo. You ever hear her speak in her own accent? She *can't*. There's thirty different personalities in there. Twenty-eight of them German.'

'So you think maybe my condition might lend itself to . . .'

'No. I think it might lend itself to an electric shock or two.'

'You're serious?'

'Deadly. But don't worry. It's quite painless.'

'The word *shock* seems to suggest that it isn't.'

'Oh no, it's not that kind of a shock. It's more like a surprise.'

'Electric surprise treatment?'

'Sure. It's like you meet someone in the street you haven't seen for a long time. Maybe they've changed. It's a shock. A surprise. Believe me, Mohammed, I'm a doctor, in your case medication's a waste of time and money. Much better just to plug you into the mains.'

'I really don't like the sound of this.'

Tarantino slapped his thighs. 'That's what they said about The Beatles! Now look at them. C'mon, Mohammed, don't look so scared. You think a toaster gets frightened every time someone shoots the juice to it? Relax. It's quite a simple procedure.'

'I'm sorry, but I'm not convinced. Besides, I'm only a wee boy. You have to ask permission.'

'Mohammed, if you're big enough to take cocaine, you're big enough to handle a few thousand volts. What's the difference? A buzz is a buzz is a buzz. You turned to drugs to try and block out things, didn't you? This'll do it permanently.'

'I turned to drugs to get high. I don't want to do this.'

'Nonsense, of course you do.'

'No, I don't.'

'You're not well, Mohammed.'

'I'm fine now.'

'You think covering walls in shit is normal?'

'No . . .'

'You think shooting Arabs, not to mention camels, is the action of a balanced individual?'

'They . . .'

'You think starving yourself near to death because you were too shy to point out it was a misunderstanding, you think that's something to be proud of?'

'No . . .'

'And you think having sexual fantasies about the prime minister of Great Britain isn't absolute proof? I've seen her, woof, woof . . .'

'I never had . . .'

'It's the final nail in your coffin, Mohammed, or it could be. Take it like a man, Mohammed. Take it before it's too late. Before you go over the edge and we can't get you back. Look at Larry, it did him the world of good.'

Mo looked at the empty bed beside him. He shook his head. There was too much . . . and not enough. There was darkness and there was light. There was sitting at the bottom of that pool and thinking about a desert. There had been a sexual fantasy about Tin Knickers. But he hadn't told anyone. Or had he? If proof was ever needed that he was a psycho, there it was. Not fantasising it, but confessing it. Tarantino was right. When it was all listed like that, he *was* a psycho.

I am evil.

I am disturbance.

Everything I touch turns to shite.

'Okay,' he said, 'if you're absolutely sure.'

'Bingo,' said Tarantino.

They strapped him in. Attached wires to his head and his hands. They wore rubber gloves. 'Think of it like you're an astronaut,' said the nurse, 'wired to the moon.'

'You do this often?' Mo asked.

'All the time,' said the nurse. 'You ought to see our electricity bill.'

'And does it work?'

'Of course it does,' she said. She handed him a

battered paperback book. It was *Portrait of the Artist as a Young Man*. 'Just a little something to make you sleep.' She cackled, and took it back off him. He blinked uncomprehendingly and she came back at him with a syringe and spiked him.

He stared for several moments at a box sitting on a table across the way from him. A metal box with wires coming from it, like the transformer box on the model railway his father used to have running through the sand in the camp in Libya. The train they used to blow up with a fingernail's worth of explosive. Not just for fun. For practice. Mo loved it. It was like *Lawrence of Arabia*.

Things were starting to get hazy.

Tarantino hovered over the box. Except it wasn't *Lawrence* any more, it was *The Bridge on the River Kwai*. The mad colonel at the end, running across the river and getting wounded by shrapnel and falling on the detonator and blowing up the bridge. Mo twitched. There was a drip of sweat on Tarantino's brow. Mo watched it make its way onto his nose and run down it like it was a ski jump, except it got to the end and sat there, frightened of the drop. Tarantino's finger traced the outline of the transformer box. 'We ready there?' he asked anxiously.

'Ready here,' said the nurse, and smiled at Mo.

'Okay,' said Tarantino, his finger resting on the switch, 'power to the people. Let's go.'

He was just in the act of flicking it when there was a voice from the door. Mo looked groggily up. Tarantino hesitated. Another nurse with a file in her hand. 'Oh, Doctor, before you blast him, we need some parental consent here.' She tapped the file.

Tarantino turned from the transformer and growled, *'What?'*

'We need permission from his parents. He's only fifteen.'

'Fourteen and a half,' said Mo.

'His parents are dead,' Tarantino snapped.

'A guardian, then. Whoever's paying the bills.'

'Well who's paying the goddamn bills?' Tarantino barked.

'Let me see,' said the nurse. Her finger ran down the file. Then ran down it again. 'We don't seem to have a record of that.'

'Oh for God's sake,' said Tarantino. He pulled his hand away from the transformer and snapped the file out of her hands. His eyes raced up and down it then he slapped it back against her chest. 'You mean I've been treating him for *nothing*?'

'I can't imagine he got this far without somebody questioning it. It must be somewhere. Just . . . not here.' She blinked hopefully at Tarantino. 'We can bill him.'

'We can't bill him,' said Tarantino. 'He's only fifteen.'

'Fourteen and . . .'

'Shut *up*,' Tarantino snapped. He closed his eyes. He opened them again and said, 'You must have a guardian.'

'Or a guardian angel,' said the nurse.

Cindy, Michael Calhoon's ceramic wife, was at home watering the flowers when the nurse called. She explained the situation and said she would need a credit card number and permission to go ahead with the treatment.

'My husband isn't here right now,' said Cindy.

'But I'm sure there won't be a problem. You just go right ahead. If the doctor says that's what he needs, well that's just fine with me. Just you hold on one second and I'll go get that credit card. American Express okay?'

A few minutes after she put the phone down, Calhoon came home for lunch. She'd made him a Caesar salad. Or at least unwrapped it. He sat staring at it. She said, 'What's wrong with you?'

'I'm worried about Mo,' he said. He was. Mo'd gone AWOL before, but there was something different about this. Sid Spielberg had called, all fired up because Jimmy Fox had dropped dead with a heart attack and wanted to know what Mo had said to upset him. But there was no sign of the boy.

'What's to worry about?' asked Cindy. 'That kid's trouble.'

'I know he's trouble,' Calhoon said softly, 'but I'm responsible for him. Besides, he's come on in leaps and bounds.'

Cindy smiled. 'Relax. He's fine. The hospital called.'

'The hospital!'

'Relax. He's fine. He fell in a swimming pool, nearly drowned. They just called to get permission.'

'*Permission?* Permission for what?'

'Oh I don't know. Some treatment. They wanted your credit card number.'

'What!'

'Relax! It wasn't much. But if you ask me, a kid of that age getting electrolysis just proves he's crazy. Still, if it keeps him out of *our* hair . . .'

Calhoon was out of his chair and out of his door and into his car before Cindy had finished laughing at her own joke.

22

Sid Spielberg brought the Porsche, with Michael Calhoon in the passenger seat and the three poodles yelping in the back. There wasn't much room for an invalid. Mo ended up sitting on Calhoon's knee with his head stuck out of the window.

'Hollywood,' Sid was saying, cigar rammed between crowned teeth, 'is littered with casualties. Montgomery Clift. James Dean. John Belushi. Biopics come a dime a dozen, and that's about what they make. The last thing we need at the end of *The Mohammed Maguire Story* is a stiff. We need a happy ending, Mo. Tell me, just tell me, what would make you happy?'

'A puppy,' said Mo.

Michael Calhoon shifted uncomfortably. Mo was too big to have his head patted. And too bizarre to be reasoned with. He had changed so much from the innocent little tyke he'd embarrassed himself in front of on the road to Belfast. It was the hunger strike, of course, something to do with starving the brain of . . . food. Energy. Vitamins. Burgers. Right from the first moment he'd staggered down the steps of the jumbo at LAX burbling about being saved by Tin Knickers, Calhoon knew that something wasn't quite right.

Something? *Everything.*

And how could it not be?

Mo was as brave as brave could be, but living with as brave as brave could be was becoming a right pain in the neck. Cindy had given him an ultimatum. Get the kid out by the end of the month, or I'm outta here.

'But I promised to adopt him.'

'So unpromise.'

'We could foster him.'

'No way.'

'Okay. Just somewhere to put his head for a few months. Just until he gets himself together.'

'He's smoking pot in the garage and pissing in the bidet. One month from now he'll be smoking pot in the bidet and pissing in the garage. I can't go on like this. I love you, Michael Calhoon, but I don't love your kid, and he ain't your kid.'

'Where are we going?' Mo said, aware that they'd missed the turn-off for the ambassador's residence.

'My place,' said Sid. 'We got you a surprise.'

'You got me a puppy?' Mo asked.

'Not quite,' said Calhoon. It had taken some arranging, and out of his own pocket as well. And now that he had started the ball rolling, it just wasn't going to stop. Not for the foreseeable future anyway. Maybe, *maybe*, he'd get it back through his ten per cent commission on *The Mohammed Maguire Story*, if only Sid would get his finger out.

If it seemed like clutching at straws, well that's what it was. But anything was better than seeing Mo lying vacant-eyed and burnt-scalped in that hospital bed.

He'd arrived at the hospital too late to stop the procedure.

But the procedure had stopped itself. Calhoon didn't fully understand how. Something to do with sweat dripping off the doctor's nose into the electrics and shorting the system. They'd managed just one short, sharp blast before everything had gone to hell. Mo had flexed against it, let out an agonised scream, and then Calhoon had crashed through the door to find Mo's hair on fire and thick black smoke filling the room, nurses flapping about crazy-eyed and the doctor struggling with a fire extinguisher.

And then when the panic had died down, Calhoon had gripped Mo's cold hand and stared fearfully at the shallow movement of his chest and asked the doctor if anything could be done.

'Well, the transformer's fucked and there's three tiles missing from the ceiling, but we can probably sort that out. There'll be smoke damage to the . . .'

'Not the fixtures and fittings! Jesus Christ, man, the boy!'

Tarantino was taken aback. He looked down at Mo. 'His hair's singed.'

'He's unconscious!'

'He's bored.'

'He's in a coma!'

'He's asleep.'

The doctor lifted Mo's hand and felt for a pulse. Then he leant in towards him. He raised one of Mo's eyelids. Then another. He stepped back and nodded. To himself, and then to Calhoon. 'MOHAMMED!' he shouted at the top of his voice and Mo shot up out of the bed.

'What . . . what . . .!' Mo yelled. 'What's burning?'

'You were,' said Tarantino, 'but we put you out.'

Mo's hands went gingerly to his head. 'Did you . . .?'

'One out of seven, completely useless,' Tarantino whined regretfully. 'But we'll have it fixed in a second.'

'You'll do nothing of the sort!' Calhoon fumed.

He turned, took one look at the smouldering transformer, then swept it off the table with his arm. 'I swore to Tin Knickers I'd keep you safe and sound, Mo, and that's just what I intend to do! You think I can phone her up and tell her I let them boil your brain like a cabbage! Not bloody likely! Right! Let's have you out of here.' He gripped Mo's arm and pulled him off the operating table.

Michael Calhoon, the Irish ambassador to Hollywood, marched his charge Mohammed Maguire, the son of two of the world's most feared terrorists, deceased, out of one hospital and into another for eight days of rest and recuperation without fear of electrocution.

They pulled into Sid's drive. 'You go ahead,' Sid said to Mo, 'round the back, beside the pool. I trust I don't have to provide arm bands.'

Mo wrinkled his brow at him and said, 'What's going on?'

Calhoon said, 'Go see.'

Mo shrugged and sauntered round the back of

the house. The sun was beating out of the heavens and he still felt weak from the electric shock. He wasn't sure if it had done his head any good, but he could recharge batteries just by sucking them. There was a sheen off the pool that hurt his eyes and he blinked away from it to the shade where someone had drawn up the sun lounger and was even now bending over trying to pick up a newspaper that had come apart and was blowing away in the breeze.

Mo put his foot out and stamped down on a fleeing page. He looked down. It was the *Belfast Telegraph*. There was a colour photograph of Tar McAdam. The headline spat: TAR ARRESTED WITH ARSENAL. Mo shuddered and prayed it didn't mean the football team.

He looked up. 'Granda,' he said.

His granda smiled and said, 'Hello. Who're you?'

'Mo,' said Mo.

His granda nodded and they looked at each other for several moments. He was wearing polka-dot bathing trunks. Folds of flaccid yellow flesh hung over the waist; not fat, just gravity-sagged ripples that had dropped off the ribs that sat out on his chest like he'd swallowed a birdcage. He wore sunglasses with a tiny white price tag still attached.

'Mo who?' his granda said eventually.

Mo looked back to the end of the pool, where Calhoon and Sid Spielberg and his three poodles had appeared. 'I don't want to seem ungrateful,' Mo said, 'but can I exchange him for the puppy?'

Calhoon looked crestfallen. Spielberg shrugged and lit another cigar.

From the other side of the pool a voice said, 'You think you've got problems? I had to fly three thousand miles with the senile oul' bastard.'

It was Harmony Hair Spray.

It was a clingfilm kiss.

It was Mary.

23

Fish fingers that were burnt on one side and still frozen on the other were a delicacy you could get in few houses along the Falls Road, and even fewer on a scorching day in Beverly Hills. Granda couldn't remember who Mo was, but he knew he liked fish fingers. They were his speciality and he insisted on making them. He'd brought them with him from Belfast. Findus Fish Fingers. Smuggled them in the fingers of his gloves because although it didn't actually specify fish fingers there was an international treaty that outlawed the transportation of certain foodstuffs between continents without the right paperwork. All the way over in the plane he wore his gloves. The air hostesses were quite concerned. They offered him extra blankets, but all the time *his* fingers were fists and his glove's fingers were frozen fish. It really pissed Mary off. They felt sorry for him because he was old and cold, and glowered at her because she smelled of fish.

Mo sat holding Mary's hand. Their feet were in the pool. Mo had removed his shoes. She touched his cheek with her other hand. 'You haven't really gone mental on me, have you, Mo?'

Mo shrugged.

She squeezed his hand. 'I didn't come all this way to kiss a nutter.'

He looked up at her, and there were tears in his eyes. She smiled and her mouth moved in towards his and her lips, red and soft, kissed him, and his mouth instinctively dropped open to receive the package. She moved her free hand up to his jaw and closed it slightly. As she did her tongue slipped through the gap and said hello to his.

'Fish fingers,' said his granda.

'Aw,' said Sid, 'don't you just love a happy ending.'

'Sure,' said Calhoon, 'she's going home tomorrow.'

'Shit,' said Sid. 'Still, no matter. *We* have a happy ending.'

Calhoon smiled and put his arm round the older man. 'Sid, I think this is the beginning of a beautiful friendship.'

Sid removed the arm. 'Mikey, with lines like that, you ain't gonna get nowhere in this business.'

They were in McDonald's. A life-size model of Ronald McDonald sat at the table beside them. Mary had a Big Mac and fries. Mo had a milkshake. 'Is it true about Tar?' Mo asked. 'He was arrested?'

'Tar's always being arrested.'

'So they won't put him away?'

'No, they probably will. It won't make any difference. He'll still be running the show.'

'He's not my number one fan.'

'No, he isn't.'

'Does he still want me dead?'

Mary nodded. 'In fact. He sent me out to do it.' She reached into her handbag. Mo sat back from his milkshake. A pink dribble ran down his chin. She pulled out a brush and ran it through her hair. 'Got you,' she said.

He smiled wistfully. 'I can't ever go back, can I?'

Mary shrugged.

'Everybody hates me,' Mo said.

She touched his hand. 'Not everybody.'

'They think I betrayed Ireland.'

'You *did* betray Ireland.'

'Oh. I thought you might . . .'

'Mo, you do what you have to do. It doesn't mean I don't love you.'

'You love me?'

'Of course I love you. I just wish I didn't have to go home tomorrow.'

'What?' said Mo.

'I'm sorry. I've exams. Your granda needed a hand.'

'You came out just to help *him*?'

'No, Mo, I came out to see you.'

'Then stay.'

'I can't.'

'Please!'

'I have to go back, Mo. I'd love to stay. But I can't.'

'*Please.*'

'Let's enjoy this, Mo, okay? I *have* to go back.'

'You don't *have* to do anything.'

'I do. I promised him I'd . . .'

'You promised who? Calhoon? I can talk to him, get him to . . .'

'Tar,' said Mary.

'*Tar?*'

'There's still work to be done, Mo. It won't be over until we've driven the last Brit out of Ireland.'

'Mary!'

'Mo!' She shook her head and peered into his eyes. 'Mo, listen to me. You have to stay here. You have to get better. You have to build yourself up and build a life for yourself. *Here*. You can't go back. They'll kill you, and I don't want them to kill you, because you're beautiful.'

'Oh,' said Mo.

Mary smiled. 'And there's one thing I have to do before I go home.'

'What's that?'

'Shag you.'

Mo laughed. 'You can't shag me. I'm fourteen and a half.'

'Mohammed Maguire. You've broken every law in the book. You're not going to get all shy on me now just because you're under age.'

'Well, put like that,' said Mo.

Three months later they buried his grandfather on a hill overlooking the city. It was perhaps only fitting that he should choke to death on a fish finger.

At least that was how Mo imagined it for his latest screenplay. In truth he died a horrible gurgling cancerous death and Calhoon had to fork out for the hospital treatment. He was cremated and there was only Mo and Sid at the service and afterwards they took his ashes and scattered them off a pier at Redondo Beach.

'He always dreamt of coming to America,' Mo said as they watched the seagulls poke their bills inquisitively into the torched remains of his grandfather as they bobbed on the soft waves. 'Do you think he was aware he made it in the end?'

Calhoon nodded against the sea breeze. Sid had refused to come out on the pier for fear of his poodles conspiring to drag him over the edge and drown him. He remained with them on the beach, being pulled this way and that. They could hear him shouting to watch out for the waves.

'He's not going to make the movie, is he?' Mo said.

Calhoon shook his head slowly. 'I don't think so, Mo.'

'He's all tit and no trousers.'

'Something like that.'

'I do like him. But I have an overwhelming urge to kill his poodles.'

'So have I,' said Calhoon. They were quiet for several minutes. There was a little smile on Mo's face. It had been there for months. It wasn't altogether appropriate for such a sad funereal day, but nobody was complaining. Calhoon was just happy that Mo was happy.

'I love all this,' Mo said.

'I know.'

'The sea and the sand and the heat and not being scared.' He took a deep breath of it. 'You know, I used to have a friend called Sandy. Tar McAdam killed him. I'd like to have shown him this.' Mo laughed suddenly.

'What?' said Calhoon.

'He would have taken one look at me and said, You're a changed man since you got your hole.'

'He's right though.'

'Aye. I suppose.'

As far as Calhoon was aware, there had been no drugs. He preferred to think that whatever madness had descended on his charge had abruptly lifted with the arrival of the little girl from Belfast rather than with the arrival of several thousand volts of electricity. He supposed he would never really know. He pictured her again: with her short hair and her T-shirt and black leggings and her wide, sharp smile. Perhaps she wasn't so little after all.

'I'm going to get you an apartment, Mo. Somewhere you can write. Near the beach, maybe. What do you think?'

'Yeah, that would be nice.' He looked up into the ambassador's face. 'You've been very kind to me, Mr Calhoon. I've never asked you why.'

'Money,' Calhoon said and smiled back out into the ocean.

24

'Yeah,' Mo admitted after quite a while, 'I suppose it *is* about the bear.'

There were spotlights coming up from below to illuminate their predicament, and indeed increase their predicament, because they could not face the glare and looked away, taking their concentration off their footing and the drop and allowing them to relax as if they were on a stage playing to an audience rather than on a ledge gambling with their lives.

Mo's feet were frozen. He had on a pair of trainers. There were holes in the sole, and indeed, holes in his soul.

He hugged the bear.

He had returned not so much in triumph as incognito.

Nine years. He had waited in vain for Mary to return, but she had not come. He had not wanted to contact her in case it got her into trouble with Tar.

Michael Calhoon was recalled to Ireland. Fluctuations in the exchange rate and changes in the tax concessions made it unfeasible for the studios to invest in Irish productions. His wife had been to Dublin on a rain-soaked vacation with him and was not enthused by the idea of going back; lucky for her she got lured away by a ceramic tile mogul and had packed her bags and left within a week of Calhoon breaking the news. He didn't mind. He'd known all along that it wasn't love, or that it was only love of crusty loaves, and after a while you got tired of crusty loaves, or they turned blue.

There was a tearful farewell with Mo at the airport. Calhoon was very proud of the way Mo was turning out and rightly took some credit for it. He wasn't a boy any more. He was a man. He'd shot up and muscled out. He was tanned and outgoing and confident, and you wouldn't know to look at him that there had been such dark times. They hugged and promised to visit, but as soon as Calhoon stepped on the plane he began to fade away from Mo's life.

Mo went to college. There was a screenwriting course and he graduated with honours. He wrote a couple of TV episodes for David Hasselhoff. They weren't very good, he knew that, but they paid well. There was a screenplay that everybody loved. It was about a boy discovering a path away from violence by learning to read and write. 'It's TV,' said the studios. 'It's a movie,' said the TV people. 'It's crap,' said Sid Spielberg before offering to buy it, 'but we can put in a car chase and a rape and then we're laughing, metaphorically speaking.'

He lived with a girl for a while at Long Beach. She surfed, he wrote. It was a perfect combination until she drowned. At least that's the way he wrote it, but in reality she met another surfer and moved on. She was unsettled by Mo's nightmares and didn't appreciate waking up in the middle of the night with a knife at her throat. You could take the boy out of the desert, but you couldn't always take the desert out of the man.

He was in love, but not with her.

One day a letter arrived. It was from a solicitor in Belfast informing him that his granda's home, the tiny slum terrace that had been left to him and that he rented out for a pittance, had been made the subject of a compulsory purchase order and was to be knocked down for a new housing estate. Did he want to contest the matter or accept the cash? When he looked at the date at the top he saw that it had been posted several months earlier. So there was probably some money to be picked up.

He loved America, and he hated Ireland, but he had to go home, and here at last was a flimsy-as-wet-tissue excuse.

He knew they had long memories, but they had

memories of a little orphan with shite in his pants. Not a grown man. He wouldn't stay. He just wanted to look and see and feel. He wanted to know what had happened to him.

On a hot December afternoon he caught a bus to LAX and then flew to London under the name of his adopted father, Michael Calhoon. He caught the Belfast shuttle and walked confidently into Aldergrove airport an hour later. He was not peered at. He was not forced to stand over a mirror so that they could check his buttocks for surface-to-air missiles. The world had moved on and Northern Ireland was at peace, after a fashion. There was a ceasefire, but people were still being killed. It was a contradiction in terms. It was home.

Mo had some money saved from his scripts for David Hasselhoff. He rented an apartment on the Malone Road. Just for a month. It was a chic address, for Belfast, but not a particularly nice apartment. He immediately had an odd feeling of déjà vu about it, but it was only after he'd been there for a few days that he realised he'd burgled it a lot of years before. That somewhere, *somewhere*, Sandy had probably left his mark.

He eased himself in. He walked the city centre. He shopped, he drank in popular bars and chatted easily. He used his American accent and was welcomed and patronised in equal measures, but not recognised. There were new shopping malls and fast food outlets familiar from his adopted home. There were bouncy playgrounds and great big concert halls hosting international stars. Everybody seemed happy. He called with his solicitor and signed some papers and collected a modest cheque. The solicitor looked at him and remembered the headlines and the photographs of the emaciated boy being removed from the prison. 'Got your appetite back then,' he said, and then coloured when there was no responsive smile.

Two days later he took a bus out to the Falls, or what was left of it. His granda's street was a sea of mud set out with foundations, like the Somme with planning permission. At one end of it the builders had completed the first phase of their redevelopment, the show houses they could show off to prospective buyers. Mo picked his way through the building site as best he could, leaping from broken slab to up-ended breezeblock. Halfway across a BMW churned past him, spraying him with mud. A van with *Belfast Telegraph* written on the side followed behind.

As Mo drew closer the din of the cement mixers and punch of the jackhammers ceased. A crowd had gathered around the BMW and a couple of camera flashes went off. The onlookers swelled about the car door as it was opened, but then parted, making way for the man who climbed out and began to make his way towards the closest of the houses, its brass front door knocker tied with a pink ribbon, shaking hands and waving greetings as he slowly progressed. From the back Mo could see that he was wearing a gold chain of office.

Mo joined the crowd. He looked at the house. Neat and freshly painted. Not necessarily any more spacious than his granda's but new and functional; no outside toilet, no leaking roof or broken floor-boards, no footprints tattooed into the front door from soldiers come looking for guns. Somebody was making a speech. A civil servant. He was thanking the Lord Mayor of Belfast for taking time out of his busy schedule to come and open the first house on the new Falls Park estate. He invited the mayor forward to say a few words. 'Ladies and gentlemen,' he said, 'our Lord Mayor, Tar McAdam.'

There was loud applause.

And only that could cover the sound of Mo's heart.

Oh no, oh Jesus no.

No. They wouldn't. They couldn't.

Mo pushed through the crowd.

He needed to see. He needed to be sure.

There were growls as he pushed, but he ignored them.

The man was talking. The man with the little beard and the tweed suit and the pipe ready in his hands.

The killer.

The gangster.

The terrorist.

The mayor.

He felt dizzy. There were words, but he could

not hear them. There was applause. There was a woman beside Tar, smiling up at him. She had a little girl beside her. Tar put his arm around them both and it prompted more applause.

It was Mary.

Mary!

'No!'

They turned.

Security men in tight suits turned, scanned, began to move towards him.

'No! Mary!'

Frightened eyes. And then her mouth fell slightly open.

'No!'

He began to move back through the crowd.

The security men began to converge.

He broke through the last line.

He began to run, fell, splattered into the mud, heaved himself up, kept running, running, running.

No. Not Mary. Not like this. Not like this!

'Oh sure, Tar's a fine upstanding gentleman now,' Inspector Campbell was saying. 'You have to give him that. Sooner or later you get tired of killing people. You grow up. There are very few middle-aged terrorists. It's a young man's game.'

Mo had his eyes closed. 'But after all the things he did. Jesus.'

'Jesus indeed,' said Mr Clarke, 'you have to forgive and forget.'

'You have to move on,' said Santa. 'And he's been a very good mayor. Great Lord Mayor's Parade. Great floats. Good uniforms. Better than this crap,' he said, pulling at his beard.

'That's my fault,' said Mr Clarke.

'You are forgiven,' said Santa.

'So,' said Mr Clarke, 'what about the bear?'

'What about the bear?' said Mo.

'Where does he come into the equation?'

'Yeah, great story, Mohammed,' said Santa, 'but what about the bear?'

Mo shrugged. 'I went to the bar. I got drunk. I had a long think about what I wanted to do.'

'And you decided on suicide,' said Inspector Campbell.

'No! I was going to send the bear to Tar McAdam.'

'What?' said Santa.

'Why on earth would you . . .'

'I was going to fill it with high explosives. I was going to blow him to bits.'

'Oh,' said Inspector Campbell. 'That would be illegal.'

'It never stopped Tar,' said Mo.

'That was in the old days,' said Santa. 'Times have changed.'

'Not for me they haven't.'

'So by closing down the store,' said Mr Clarke, '*I* saved Tar McAdam's life.'

'It's nothing to be pleased about,' Mo said wearily. He sighed. 'So it was a stupid idea. You're right. The world has moved on. I just haven't moved on with it.'

Seeing her happy. Seeing *him* happy. Didn't people know? Didn't they remember? How could somebody be a psychotic killer one minute and the Lord Mayor the next? Where was the sense in it? A terrorist. A bad guy. And now a good guy. With the world at his feet and the most beautiful girl in the world in his bed.

Madness.

The Irish.

The *Northern* Irish.

So used to violence that they could forget it in the blink of an eye.

I cannot.

I cannot.

I cannot live with this.

I don't fit. I don't want to be part of a world where Tar McAdam is a good guy.

Mo peered into the darkness. He hugged the bear. Then he let it go.

It dropped. It didn't sail or float like a soft, fluffy thing.

It fell. There was an *ooooooooh* from below.

It bounced.

'I was going to kill him, but that's not the answer,' Mo said. The others had their eyes on the bear. Mo shook his head. He took a deep breath. 'I can't stand this any more. I'm ready to go over.'

Mo moved slightly forward. Now he peered at the ground. Anxious spectators had gathered around the bear. One of the spotlights had given up, and the other was weakening. He could pick out a few faces looking up at him. He turned to his companions. 'Are youse coming with me?' he asked. 'We've been out here long enough.'

There was silence. Their eyes were still on the bear.

'Have your lives noticeably improved since you climbed out?' Mo asked. 'I don't think so.'

Santa shook his head. 'Got worse, if anything.'

'It's still Christmas Eve,' Mr Clarke said, 'and my store's still closing.'

'What about you, Inspector,' Mo asked, 'you joining us?'

Inspector Campbell screwed his eyes shut. 'They'll have me working traffic after this. I can't face that.'

Mo took a deep breath. 'Okay, lads,' he said, 'let's do it.'

He did not believe in God. Never had, never would. But as he stepped over the edge he crossed himself. Everyone does.

25

And maybe it was his mother reaching out to him, or his father, or God, or a sudden shift in the wind, but he stopped, he wavered, one foot out into space, the other on the verge of joining it, easier to fall forward than to flail back. But he stopped. He managed it, just, and when they saw that he'd changed his mind they grabbed him and hauled him back to the ledge. There was a voice from below, emotive, plaintive, familiar.

'Mo! Don't do it, Mo! Mo!'

Another *ooooooh* from the remnants of the crowd below.

Mo staggered back, breathless, then leant forward, peering into the darkness.

A face.

Her face.

'*Mary?*' He felt thrilled, and frozen at the same time.

'Mo! Don't do it, Mo – please! Things aren't that bad!'

'That's easy for you to say!'

'Mo! Please!'

'I can't believe you married him!'

'Two-faced bitch!' hissed Santa.

'Shhhh,' said Mr Clarke.

'Married who?' she cried.

'Tar!'

'I didn't marry Tar!'

'I'm not blind!'

'Not yet,' said Inspector Campbell.

'Mo! Please! Go inside, please! Let's talk!'

'There's nothing to talk about!'

'There is – we love you!'

'Huh!'

'Claire loves you!'

'Who the fuck is Claire!'

'Your daughter!'

'What?'

The little girl was standing beside her. There was a policeman standing beside Mary with a megaphone in his hands. Mary grabbed it off him. She fumbled with it for several moments, then found a switch and handed it to Claire. 'Claire, love, tell your daddy what you really want for Christmas.'

Claire looked to the ledge. She thought for a moment. 'Daddy . . .' she said, 'I want a CD player, and a big doll, and a computer game . . .'

Mary grabbed the megaphone off her, mad, then raised it to her own lips. 'We love you, Mohammed Maguire. Don't do this!'

There was a semblance of a cheer from the gathered spectators.

Mo was stunned.

My daughter?

'I saw you! With Tar McAdam! She's his!'

'She's not!'

'She is!'

'Mo – this isn't the best place for this!'

'He had his arm round you! He's the mayor!'

'He was giving me the keys to the house! I was top of the queue of unmarried mothers!'

'What!'

'Mo! Please!'

'She's not mine!'

'She is! Look at her! She's the spitting image! Come down and see!' She added quickly, 'But don't jump!'

'No! *No.*' Mo looked desperately at his companions. They were fascinated.

'She does look like you,' Inspector Campbell said.

'She's miles away,' said Santa.

'I'm not sure,' said Mr Clarke.

'If she was mine you would have told me!' Mo bellowed.

'I wrote to you! You didn't reply! I thought you weren't interested. And also I would have been arrested. You were under age . . .'

'Let's not get into that now!' Mo yelled.

'I love you, Mo! Claire loves you! It's Christmas! Please, Mo! We want you back so badly.'

Could she, for one mad instant, be telling the truth?

Had there ever, ever in his life been a time when anything had gone right, or if it had, had it not also been booby-trapped?

She was down there.

The reason he'd come back.

To find out. And he'd found out.

Or jumped to a conclusion. As he'd been trying to, all day.

She was down there. With his daughter.

His daughter. *Nine years.*

Nine years. Why hadn't she tracked him down?

What did it matter? She was there. Now. With his daughter. *We want you back so badly.*

God!

He put his head back against the wall. There were tears falling now, but they weren't suicidal tears. They were tears of hope and relief. He looked at Santa and Mr Clarke and Inspector Campbell. 'Oh God,' he said, 'aren't they beautiful?'

'Not from here,' said Santa.

Mo wiped at his eyes. 'I'm sorry, lads, I can't go through with this. I have to find out. I'm sorry.' He paused. He shook his head. 'I let the bastards grind me down. But what if . . . oh God, I mean, what if she really is my daughter? What if Mary really does love me?'

'Words,' Santa said, 'to stop you jumping. She's a liar.'

'Don't be such a cynic,' said Mr Clarke. 'She sounds sincere.'

'They all sound sincere,' said Santa, 'then they stab you in the back with a rusty knife.' *His* voice was cracking.

They looked at him. 'Are you . . .?' Inspector Campbell began.

Santa cut him off. 'What? Am I not allowed feelings too? The collapse of communism may have been catastrophic, but getting dropped by your boyfriend right before Christmas hurts too.' His moist eyes burrowed into the darkness. 'Neil!' Santa called. 'I love you.'

They didn't know what to say. None of them had seen Santa crying before.

'Mo's right,' Mr Clarke said, trying to change the subject, 'we have let the bastards grind us down. We have to fight back. People lose their jobs all the time. It's not the end of the world. They're not going to starve. *I'm* not going to starve. There'll be redundancy money . . . other jobs . . . a management buy-out. Or start my own place. Quality goods, toys . . . Santa, we could get you a good uniform, proper toys . . .'

The tears were flooding down Santa's face. 'My heart's been broken . . .' He edged forward. 'I just want him to hug me.'

'He's not going to want to hug a mess of blood and bone,' said Mo.

Mr Clarke swallowed, alarmed. It was the first time he'd considered the physical consequences of hitting the pavement at a great rate of knots.

Santa shook his head. His beard was hanging loose off his chin at one corner.

Mo looked at Mr Clarke. 'I'm going in,' he said. 'What about you?'

'I'm with you,' Mr Clarke said. He leant forward to look at the inspector. 'Inspector, what about you?'

Inspector Campbell, his eyes wide with disdain, looked at Santa. 'I'm not staying out here with a fruit, people might talk.'

A sudden and renewed fury swept Santa. 'I am bloody going in!' he bellowed. 'So I can fight bigoted bastards like you!' He dragged an arm across his face and began to shuffle towards the inspector. And suddenly the inspector's legs were working again, all day frozen and now suddenly mobile, and a smile spread across his face even as Santa bore down on him. Warmth and confidence surged through his body. His master plan had worked. He had talked them in. His career was saved, and he'd probably get a medal.

Mo bent out into the darkness. 'It's okay,' he called, 'we're coming in. Wait for me, Mary! Claire! Daddy's coming home!'

There was a cheer from below. The fire chief said, 'Right, lads,' and they began to deflate the giant mattress.

Inspector Campbell arrived at the window and arms reached out to him. He clambered in.

'You won't be putting this on your CV,' Mo said to Mr Clarke, the pair of them shuffling along, then stopping behind Santa as he decided which way to manoeuvre his bulk through the narrow window.

Mr Clarke smiled. 'What, talking an unhappy customer down from a ledge? It'll do me no harm at . . .'

The ledge gave way.

They fell. Santa. Mr Clarke. Mo.

Freefall.

It seemed to take an eternity.

The ground inched towards Mo.

He saw Claire's face smiling up, like it was a dream. And Mary's mouth drop open, knowing it was not.

He saw his mother and his father, hand in hand in the sand. Kissing.

He smelled burning, burning flesh, smoke in the desert.

Gunshots and Sandy squealing.

The thwack of leather batons on naked flesh.

Sanctuary.

Sid.

Mary.

Claire

Mary, I . . .

The deflating mattress was directly beneath him now, but there was no way of telling if there was sufficient air in it to save him.